One of the good guys.

As she stared at his kind, handsome face once again, she calmed.

She didn't know if she could trust him, because she just couldn't remember much of anything. Not even her name.

But she had to start trusting someone if she was going to find out who she was and why she felt she wasn't safe.

"Okay," she said with a slow nod. "I'll go with you, but you can't leave me alone."

A ghost of a smile drifted across his lips, and he made the sign of a little cross over his heart. "I promise I won't leave you alone."

She nodded again, and the action made her head throb. She rubbed her temple and encountered the edges of the temporary bandage he'd put in place barely half an hour earlier.

He wouldn't do that if he wanted her dead, would he?

BURIED TRUTHS

CARIDAD PIÑEIRO

MIX
Paper | Supporting responsible forestry
FSC® C021394

To my wonderful daughter, Samantha Ann.
I am incredibly proud of all that you have accomplished with your writing and look forward to reading TRAVELER, your next release!

Recycling programs for this product may not exist in your area.

ISBN-13: 978-1-335-69070-8

Buried Truths

For questions and comments about the quality of this book, please contact us at CustomerService@Harlequin.com.

Harlequin Enterprises ULC
22 Adelaide St. West, 41st Floor
Toronto, Ontario M5H 4E3, Canada
www.Harlequin.com

HarperCollins Publishers
Macken House, 39/40 Mayor Street Upper,
Dublin 1, D01 C9W8, Ireland
www.HarperCollins.com

Printed in Lithuania

New York Times and *USA TODAY* bestselling author **Caridad Piñeiro** is a Jersey girl who just wants to write and is the author of nearly fifty novels and novellas. She loves romance novels, superheroes, TV and cooking. For more information on Caridad and her dark, sexy romantic suspense and paranormal romances, please visit www.caridad.com.

Books by Caridad Piñeiro

Harlequin Intrigue

Crooked Pass Security

Cliffside Kidnapping
Defended by the Bodyguard
Cold Case K-9
Buried Truths

South Beach Security: K-9 Division

Sabotage Operation
Escape the Everglades
Killer in the Kennel
Danger in Dade

South Beach Security

Lost in Little Havana
Brickell Avenue Ambush
Biscayne Bay Breach

Cold Case Reopened
Trapping a Terrorist
Decoy Training

Visit the Author Profile page at Harlequin.com.

CAST OF CHARACTERS

Mark Dillon—Regina Police Department Sergeant and K-9 handler Mark is an avid hiker familiar with the areas around Regina. He has risen through the ranks in the police department and is helping to create the new K-9 division.

Amanda/Natalie Alonso—Amanda Alonso is the CFO of a venture fund and stands accused of stealing millions from investors. Amanda is currently in the Witness Protection Program, as she is going to testify against her former boyfriend and boss. Natalie Alonso is Amanda's twin sister and a Denver homicide detective.

Rocky—Mark Dillon's K-9 partner, Rocky, is a large, black Cane Corso trained for protection and tracking.

Jackson Whitaker—The Regina Police Department Chief, Jackson is Sophie and Robbie Whitaker's cousin and is determined to bring the latest crime-solving technologies to his small-town police department.

Josefina (Sophie) Whitaker—Sophie Whitaker is a computer genius who was working with her Miami cousins at South Beach Security, but is now one of the founders of their Crooked Pass Security division. An MIT graduate, she and her older brother, Robbie, had started a business together in Silicon Beach, developing games and apps, and also doing ethical hacking before joining South Beach Security with their Gonzalez cousins.

Robert (Robbie) Whitaker—Robbie Whitaker is a computer genius who works with his younger sister, Sophie, and helped found Crooked Pass Security. He has a close relationship with Sophie, and together they rely on the latest technologies to help solve crimes and protect vulnerable people.

Chapter One

Mark Dillon approached the trailhead and paused, lifting his face to the warmth of the late-spring sun that had chased away the chill of early morning. His K-9, Rocky, a powerful black cane corso, sat at his side and copied his stance, lifting his muzzle into the air.

Mark glanced at Rocky, smiled, and rubbed the dog's large head, earning him a doggy kiss on his hand. "You're a good boy," he said. Rocky had been obedient as they'd hiked across a nearby meadow before returning to the trailhead.

He'd been training Rocky for nearly a year, and in that year, Rocky had matured into a powerful protector and a helpful partner in search and rescue operations.

But as obedient as he was, he needed a lot of activity to keep him in shape and, more importantly, happy.

Today's hike was the perfect way to do that, especially since it was such a gorgeous day.

The nearby meadow was a carpet of thick, verdant grass broken by patches of purple clematis and penstemon, bright yellow wallflowers, and taller, almost bush-like butterfly weed plants. They were true to their word since several vibrant butterflies flitted around the blossoms.

By a burbling creek running through the meadow, the greens and purples of mountain bluebells and tall, hairy leaves of cow parsnip shot from the dark, fertile ground.

Ahead of him, along the trail, assorted trees had bloomed, painting the mountainside bright green.

Beautiful, he thought. It was why he loved hiking the woods and meadows in his spare time. Not to mention that his detailed knowledge of the areas around town had proved useful in more than one recent investigation.

It was why he had become his police chief's right-hand man and the sergeant responsible for building a new K-9 division together with Diego Rodriguez, an agent with Crooked Pass Security in Denver.

With a soft click under his tongue to Rocky, they hiked the trail, an intermediate one that would challenge the canine and provide the activity he needed.

They had barely gone a hundred yards when something crashed through the nearby underbrush, snaring his attention. Fear chilled his gut that it might be a bear or bobcat.

He shortened Rocky's leash, pulled him close, and commanded him to stay in German. *"Bleib."*

He reached for the bear spray before realizing it wasn't anything dangerous.

It was a woman, a beautiful woman, bruised and bloodied, struggling to walk through the underbrush. Her arms were wrapped tightly around herself to stay warm because she wore only a short-sleeved blouse and jeans. Not enough protection with the early morning chill.

He reinforced the stay command to Rocky and rushed to help the woman, who had stumbled and fallen to her knees, crying. But he wasn't sure if she was crying in relief or despair.

When he reached her, he said, "You're okay. I'm a police officer."

She flinched, backed away from him, and whimpered, "No, no, no."

Not the reaction he expected.

Holding his hands up in pleading, he reassured her. "You're safe. Let me help."

He slipped off his jacket and wrapped it around the woman.

She peered up at him, eyes slightly unfocused, and clumsily slipped it on. As she poked her arms through the sleeves, the bright pink-red ligature marks at her wrists stood out against her pale skin.

He muttered a curse beneath his breath, and she jerked back, fearful once again.

SHE CRAB-CRAWLED back a few inches, afraid of the man.

He'd said he was a cop. She didn't know why that scared her more than comforted.

But he had kind, amazing green eyes in a youthful, handsome face. He was probably only in his late twenties.

Not much older than…

How old am I? she wondered for a hot second before he said, "What's your name?"

She opened her mouth to answer but couldn't.

She shook her head, both in denial and as if that might shake loose the response, but it didn't.

"I don't know," she said as a shiver wracked her body despite the warmth of his jacket. It still held his body heat and smelled nice. Masculine and clean.

"Do you know where you are?" he asked as he helped her to her feet.

"Thank you," she said because the ground had been cold and slightly damp. The morning sun had yet to pierce the tree leaves and warm the earth.

He didn't release her hand, steadying her as they picked their way to the hard-packed trail she had spotted earlier that morning. She had been trying to reach it in the hope of…

What had she been hoping? To escape? she asked herself even as he once again asked, "Do you know where you are?"

She wanted to curse at him that she was on the side of a mountain with a stranger and a massive black dog that looked more like a bear, but held back. He seemed to be trying to help.

"You're bleeding," he said.

She reached up to the warmth on her forehead and encountered sticky wetness.

As she brought her hand down, she stared at the cherry-red blood on her fingers, and her knees buckled slightly.

He slipped an arm around her waist, offering support, and she reacted, driving her foot down on his instep and jabbing his solar plexus, drawing a grunt from him.

"Easy. I'm just trying to help," he said, echoing her thoughts.

"I can take care of myself," she said and instantly felt stupid.

She was lost on an unknown trail, cold and bleeding, and she couldn't even remember her name, much less anything else. Except that maybe she couldn't trust the police.

"We need to go to the hospital," he said, and despite her aggression, offered his support to clear the last tangle of underbrush.

She didn't think the hospital was a good idea. She didn't know why. She just knew she should be somewhere…

She didn't know where, she thought with another shake of her head that made it ache.

"I'm okay. I just want to go…" Her voice trailed off as it hit her once again that she didn't know…anything.

It was obvious to Mark that she had some kind of amnesia. Probably from the head wound.

That, together with her other assorted bumps and bruises, said that a trip to the hospital was necessary.

The ligature marks on her wrists also confirmed that this wasn't just a run-of-the-mill hiking injury. Especially since only weeks earlier, Colorado Bureau of Investigation agents and Crooked Pass Security had helped arrest a serial killer responsible for several abductions and murders not far from here.

Because of that, he took out his phone and dropped a pin to mark the location so that a crime scene unit could scour the area for evidence.

"We're going to the hospital," he said in a tone that brooked no disagreement. He clicked his tongue, and Rocky immediately came to their side.

The woman glanced at the dog and went to rub his head, but then drew her hand back as if realizing Rocky wasn't a pet.

"He's my partner," Mark said and quickly tacked on, "His name is Rocky. Like the boxer. I'm Mark. And you're…"

"Empty," she said with a wealth of sadness in her voice and gaze as it settled on his face. "I can't remember anything."

He gestured to her head wound. "It's probably just temporary. Let's get you cleaned up and then go see a doctor."

She gratefully didn't argue, walking beside him to where he had parked his Jeep Wrangler.

He helped her into the passenger seat and pulled out a first aid kit and a thermos from his backpack. After pouring some coffee into the lid that doubled as a cup, he handed it to her.

She accepted the coffee with shaky hands and sipped it before saying, "Thank you."

Polite despite the instep stomp and gut punch. "You're welcome. Could you turn toward me?"

She did as he asked, slightly more pliant, and he quickly opened the first aid kit and cleaned the small cut at her hairline. After, he did his best to put on a butterfly bandage, thinking she might need a stitch or two.

Because she seemed to be enjoying the coffee, he skipped asking about the marks on her wrists. Besides, he wanted the doctor and his police chief to confirm that they were ligature marks.

"The hospital isn't far. I just need to get Rocky harnessed," he said, and she nodded and turned so he could close the door.

With a hand gesture, he instructed Rocky to hop into the back seat and secured him for the short ride to their small local hospital in Regina.

As he hopped into the driver's seat, he reached for his phone to call his chief, but given her earlier response to his saying he was a police officer, he held back. There would be enough time while a doctor examined her.

Because she was skittish, he tried to keep her informed of what he was doing as he pulled out of the parking lot.

"We're not far from the hospital in Regina. Have you ever been to Regina?" he said as he drove to the main highway.

She hunched her shoulders, the movement almost imperceptible beneath the down of his jacket on her petite body. "I don't know," she said and sipped the coffee again.

"It's a pretty town. Main Street is like a postcard," he said, keeping his tone friendly.

With another shrug, she said, "I wouldn't know. My brain is empty."

Her last words were filled with pain and tore at his heart.

He laid a hand on her arm, offering comfort. "It'll come back, and we'll keep you safe until it does."

She met his gaze for a heartbeat before he returned his attention to the road. Her gaze had been filled with doubt, pain, and fear. A maelstrom of emotions.

Her next words confirmed his reading of her state.

"I don't know who to trust."

He stroked his hand down her arm again and said, "You can trust me."

"You're a cop," she said as if *cop* was a dirty word.

With another quick glance in her direction, he said, "How about you think of me as plain ol' Mark?"

He felt her gaze on him for long moments before she let out

a strangled laugh and said, “I’m not sure anyone can call you plain or old.”

He chuckled. “Okay. Just Mark, then.”

“Just Mark,” she said with a playful laugh and shake of her head.

Minutes later, he pulled into the lot for the hospital and drove straight to the emergency room entrance.

As he parked, an almost animal-like keening built from deep inside her.

“I can’t go in there. He’ll find me. He’ll hurt me,” she said and tossed the last of her coffee at him.

Chapter Two

The lukewarm liquid hit him full in the face, stunning him for a second, but not long enough for her to escape.

He shot an arm out to force her back against the seat and keep her from opening the door.

"Who will hurt you?" he asked, wondering if her memory was returning so she could offer him something they could work with.

She shook her head again and tried to pry his arm away. "I don't know. I only know it's not safe in public. I have to hide," she said, and her gaze darted all around, as if she were searching for some kind of hidey-hole or a possible attacker.

"I will keep you safe. I won't leave you alone," he said as she struggled against his hold.

She stopped then and met his gaze full-on. "How do I know that? How can I trust you?"

With a shrug of his shoulders and a shake of his head, he said, "Trust is a lot like faith. You just have to believe I'm one of the good guys."

One of the good guys.

As she stared at his kind, handsome face once again, she calmed.

She didn't know if she could trust him because she just couldn't remember much of anything. Not even her name.

But she had to start trusting someone if she was going to find out who she was and why she felt she wasn't safe.

"Okay," she said with a slow nod. "I'll go with you, but you can't leave me alone."

A ghost of a smile drifted across his lips, and he made the sign of a little cross over his heart. "I promise I won't leave you alone."

She nodded again, and the action made her head throb. She rubbed her temple and encountered the edges of the temporary bandage.

He wouldn't do that if he wanted me dead, would he?

Trust him, said the little voice in her head as he left the driver's seat and walked around to unharness Rocky. When he opened her door, she tamped down the instinct to run even though her gut had gone cold and her heart pounded in her chest.

She had to trust him.

Besides, she had nowhere to run.

He held his hand out to help her down, and she hesitated, but then slipped her hand into his.

As her feet hit the ground, her knees almost buckled, but he was there, strong and steady. The feel of his sturdy, muscled arm was welcome this time and calmed the nervous beat of her heart.

With Rocky at their side, they walked the short distance to the doors of the ER, which slid open as they approached. Inside, it was relatively quiet with only a duo of patients in chairs. A young boy with a tear-stained face held his arm while his mother comforted him. An older woman coughed into a handkerchief, a deep, unhealthy rattle in her chest.

The nurse stationed at the ER desk popped up as they walked in.

"Sergeant Dillon. Why don't you take her to room number 3?" she said and gestured toward a back section of the ER area.

They shuffled over together, and once inside the room, he helped her onto the examining room table. After, he was about to walk out of the room when she called out, "You promised to stay."

He held up a hand, asking for calm. "I'm just going to see if the doctor's on his way, and Rocky is going to protect you."

"*Pass auf*," he said, issuing a command to the dog.

Mark had barely taken a step when a doctor came to the door. He was an elderly man with a leonine head of white hair and a beard that reminded her of Santa Claus.

"Sergeant Dillon. Who have we here?" the man said with a soft, almost beatific smile.

"She's hit her head and doesn't remember anything, Doc," Mark said and gave the dog another instruction that made Rocky heel at his side.

"All right. Is it okay if I take a look?" the doctor asked as he approached, calming her with his gentle demeanor.

She nodded, and her head throbbed again, making her wince.

"Where does it hurt?" he asked, and from the corner of her eye, she saw Mark shift away to the door of the room with Rocky, giving them some privacy while keeping his promise not to leave.

She gestured to her forehead and then to the back of her head, where there was a large goose egg she realized as she lightly pressed her hand there.

The doctor gently probed the area, parting her hair so lightly she almost didn't feel it. Then he was delicately peeling away Mark's bandage and reviewing his handiwork. "Mark did a good job. Those butterfly bandages are all you need," he said, but also lightly touched the area, checking for more damage.

"Anywhere else?" he asked.

Truth be told, her body was starting to ache in multiple places now that the fight-or-flight response was ebbing.

"Everywhere," she admitted with a harsh laugh.

"Would you mind if I got a nurse in here to help you undress so I can take a better look?"

She glanced at Mark nervously, and seemingly understanding, he said, "We'll stay at the door. We won't leave."

Meeting the doctor's concerned gaze, she nodded and said, "Okay."

MARK STOOD GUARD with Rocky, waiting for Doc Martin and Nurse Sampson to finish their examination.

They'd only been in there a few minutes, so he expected it might still be some time. Enough for him to call his police chief, but as he reached for his cell phone, Chief Jackson Whitaker sauntered into the emergency room and met him at the door.

"Chief," he said with a dip of his head. "I guess Nurse Nelson at the desk gave you a call."

"You guessed right. What have we got here?" he asked.

"Woman, late twenties. Head injury. Ligature marks on her wrists. Doesn't trust the police and is running from something. But she can't remember anything," Mark advised.

"Does *anything* include her name?" Jackson asked and tipped his police ball cap up slightly.

"It does, Chief," he confirmed with a nod.

"You found her on the hiking trail?" Jackson pressed.

"Off the trail, crashing through the underbrush. Thought it was a bear," he said and then quickly tacked on, "This isn't just some hiker who got lost and fell on the trail."

Jackson nodded and stared at the door, and as if on cue, the doctor stepped out.

"What can you tell us, Doc?" Jackson asked the older man.

"Head injuries. A blow to the back of the head probably knocked her out. The blow caused a slight concussion. The injury on her forehead was likely from her falling and hitting something. She also has bruising and scratches in assorted spots."

"She had been stumbling through the underbrush. Could they be from that?" Mark asked.

Doc Martin tilted his head from side to side, as if considering, and then nodded. "They would seem consistent with that. Not so much with the damage on her wrists. Restrained with zip ties."

"Can you tell how long she was on the trail? If she was there overnight?" Mark asked.

Doc Martin did that head bob again before saying, "Tough to tell. Did you have the heat on in your car?"

"I did. Her skin was cold, and she was shivering," Mark advised, recalling her earlier state.

"I can't tell from her current body temperature, but I don't see any signs of hypothermia. She's lucky you found her. She wouldn't have survived a night on the mountain with the cold nights we've been having," the doctor said.

A long silence followed, interrupted only by Nurse Sampson opening the door and a shout from the woman inside, asking, "Where's Mark?"

Mark gripped the edge of the door and said, "Are you dressed?"

"Yes," she said with a sigh of what seemed like relief.

He peered inside. She was back on the examination table and offered the barest hint of a smile as she saw him.

"My chief is here. Is it okay for him to come in?" he asked.

The smile faded, and fear crept into her gaze. She nervously plucked at the examining table sheet until he said, "He's a good guy, too."

She reluctantly nodded.

At that, Mark walked to her, Rocky at his side, and signaled for Jackson to join them.

Jackson ambled in and kept a slight distance away, aware of the woman's delicate state.

"I'm Chief Jackson Whitaker. My friends call me Jax. I understand you're having trouble remembering things," he said, his tone gentle and comforting.

"That's an understatement," she said, sarcasm dripping from her words.

Jackson shared a look with him before continuing. "We're a little worried about those marks on your wrists. Do you remember how you got them?"

She glanced at her wrists and then rubbed the redder one with a hand. With a shake of her head that sent the shoulder-length strands of her brown hair swinging, she said, "I was tied up, but I was able to get away. I gave myself room to slip free of the zip ties by putting my palms down."

Peering at them, her gaze puzzled, she said, "How did I know that?"

With a shrug, Jackson said, "A cop or soldier might know that."

"Or a woman who took a self-defense class," Mark interjected.

"Or a woman who took a self-defense class," Jackson repeated with a quick look at the young sergeant as if to ask him not to offer answers for her. "Does that seem familiar?"

The woman shook her head and stared at her wrists. "No. It doesn't."

Jackson glanced at Mark again and then at Rocky. "I think you and Rocky should take this young lady to our safe house until we know more."

"You can't ask around about me. They'll know," she said, wringing her hands together, slightly more frantic again.

Mark laid a comforting hand over hers, stilling the nervous motion. "Who'll know?" he asked, hoping she might remember.

But she only glanced at him, eyes pleading. "I don't know. I don't know," she said with a wail.

Jackson laid a hand on her shoulder, and she flinched, making him instantly retreat. "I won't ask around. It'll be just Mark and me seeing what we can find out," he said, and that seemed to calm her.

With a tilt of his head toward the door, he walked out, and Mark followed but kept the door open so the woman knew he was still there as promised.

"Let's get her prints, and I'll see if there are any hits in AFIS. Take a photo also for some facial recognition programs," he said.

"What if that triggers something? What if someone is looking for her?" Mark said, mindful of the woman's concerns about staying hidden.

Jackson tipped up the brim of his baseball cap a little more to scratch at his forehead. "You're right. Let me call Crooked Pass Security and see if they can run an untraceable search."

"Same thing for missing person reports, right? Maybe they can use their fancy software and search the web for her?" Mark said, brows raised in emphasis.

"That makes sense," Jackson said.

"Great minds," Mark teased, earning a chuckle from his boss, who was also a good friend.

"It's why I made you a sergeant, Mark. But if this is something big, which we both suspect, we need to be extra vigilant," Jackson said and shot a quick look at the woman inside the examining room.

"My bones say it's big, Jax. Real big," Mark said, and jammed his hands on his hips as he considered the frightened woman who was staring at them with wide eyes the color of Texas bluebells.

Jackson laughed and clapped him on the shoulder. "Those bones aren't old enough to know much. Mine either, especially if this is something big."

"I guess it's a good thing we can call in Crooked Pass Security," Mark said, grateful that Jackson could reach out to his tech genius cousins who ran the agency.

"Definitely a good thing. Let's get her prints and photo," he said.

They reentered the room, and Jackson handed Mark a mobile fingerprint scanner, one of the new technologies that Jackson had introduced to their police department. He hoped to bring in even more technology and services as the budget allowed, like the new K-9 division that he and Diego were working on.

Mark walked over and, after double-checking to make sure that the device was not transmitting the prints to AFIS, he asked for the young woman's right hand.

Her hand trembled as he delicately urged it onto the screen of the scanner. He recorded her fingertips and then repeated the process with her thumb, and then with her other hand.

After, he raised his cell phone and snapped a few photos of her face from various angles.

"We will secure everything. You don't need to worry about that," he said as he handed the scanner to Jackson.

Her gaze was intense as it focused on the transfer of the equipment, but then she nodded and said, "What now?"

"Rocky and I are taking you to our safe house. You can clean up, and we'll get you some fresh clothes. Make something to eat," Mark said, and helped her off the examining table.

As she had before, she hesitated and glanced between him and Jackson. "You're the good guys, right?"

At their nods, she slipped her hand into his and put on the jacket he'd given her earlier.

For safety's sake, he zipped up his jacket and lifted the collar to obscure the lower portion of her face. "Can you tuck your hair up, like girls do?" he said, circling his index finger around her long strands.

With an anxious laugh, she swept her hair into her hands and did a little twirl to make a topknot. "At least I remember that," she said.

Jackson pulled his ball cap off and handed it to her. "Can you put this on?"

She did and drew it low to hide most of her face.

"Are we good to go?" she asked.

"We're good," Mark said and clicked his tongue for Rocky to follow as they exited into the lobby for the ER.

Jackson swiped his arm out to keep them back. "Let me go first. I'll signal if it's clear."

He hated for Jackson to go first. He had a new baby, after all. But Mark was the one responsible for their mystery woman, so he nodded and let his boss lead the way.

The doors slid open, and Jackson stepped into the late-morning sun.

He peered all around, searching the parking lot before a little wave of his hand signaled it was safe.

While Jackson hurried to the squad car, Mark took the woman back to his Jeep and helped her in. After harnessing Rocky, he hopped into the driver's seat for the quick ride to the safe house, which was not far from the Regina police station.

He followed Jackson's squad car out of the parking lot and to the highway to the center of town. Barely a few minutes later, they were making the turnoff for Main Street, with the quaint shops and restaurants loved by visitors to Regina who came to ski and hike the nearby mountainside or take advantage of the beautiful lake in town to fish and engage in watersports.

As Jackson executed a K-turn to pull in front of the station, Mark continued for another few blocks and turned onto the side street where the safe house was located.

It was a small Cape Cod with a fenced-in yard that made it easier to secure.

He pulled into the driveway and parked.

"Are you good to go?" he asked the woman.

Chapter Three

If she hadn't been so afraid for her safety, she might have appreciated the lovely downtown they'd just driven through with all its charming shops and restaurants. The many spring flowers here and there in the planters along Main Street gave it a happy, joyful air.

Even this cute little Cape Cod screamed "home" more than "safe house," she thought as Mark exited the car and walked around to free Rocky from the back seat.

Colorful flowers waved happily along a paved walkway leading to the front porch of the home, where a bright blue bench swung from chains. The bench welcomed you to come and sit a spell. Slatted, wooden cubes were placed here and there, for use either as tables or additional seats.

The bench color matched that of the front door, beckoning you to approach.

Mark offered her a hand as she slipped from the Jeep, and surprisingly, she was feeling better. Steadier. Maybe it was his presence and that of Rocky, whose large, imposing stature would scare someone off, certain that the dog could inflict major damage.

She took Mark's hand and followed him to the door, which he unlocked and opened.

The beep of an alarm hinted that the home was secure, but Mark wasn't going to take any chances. He shut off the alarm, urged her in just past the door, looked at her, and said, "Let me check it out first."

"Okay," she said, although it was easy to see that the open-concept living/dining/kitchen space was clear.

Still, Mark did a quick look around and then pushed to the back of the house, which she presumed held the bedrooms and bathrooms. Or maybe just one bathroom, given the size of the home.

Seemingly satisfied, he returned, closed the door, and reset the alarm. "The code is 0307, and in case of an emergency, hit this panic button to the left. It'll trigger a silent alarm that will bring the cops on an urgent basis."

"Hopefully, we won't need that," she said, feeling safer with each minute she spent in his care.

And Rocky's, she thought, as the immense cane corso, who reached almost to mid-waist, sat beside her and licked her hand.

"He likes you," Mark said with a smile. He had a really nice smile and dimples. She'd always been a sucker for dimples.

Good. A memory, finally, silly as it was.

"Let me show you to your room," he said, and as he had before, offered her his hand and commanded Rocky to guard the door.

She didn't need his support, but the feel of his hand, strong and masculine, was comforting. And until she could remember who she was and why she felt she had to hide, she'd take all the comfort she could.

He led her to a nice bedroom done in shades of blue. The walls boasted lovely landscapes of what looked like Regina's downtown.

"Nice paintings," she said.

"Jax's wife is an artist. Well respected. She's the one who keeps this place looking pristine. She paints here occasionally for her shop in town. If I know Jax, he'll have Rhea round up some clothes and food for us."

He gestured to a door at the far side of the room. "Bathroom's over there. There's a clean robe behind the door if you want to shower."

She touched the bandage on her hairline. "What about this?"

"I can put a fresh one on once you're done."

"That sounds good," she said, savoring the idea of a nice, long, hot shower.

MARK WAITED UNTIL she had closed the bathroom door and then took a deep breath.

Not quite how he had expected his Sunday to go.

But she needed protection, and there was no one better than Rocky and him for the job.

He walked into the kitchen area and listened. The water was running in the shower, and he focused on that as he went to the coffee machine and made some coffee.

All the while, the sibilant sound of the water in the pipes accompanied him.

He suspected a long, hot shower might be what she needed to relax. Maybe enough to open some spigot in her brain so memories could spill out to help them identify her and keep her safe.

The burble of the coffee machine melded with the sound of the streaming water until the latter finally stopped.

He waited, aware he'd have to redo the butterfly bandage, but wanting to give her the privacy to towel down and slip into the robe.

The minutes seemed long, maybe too long, which prompted him to walk to the bedroom door and listen.

Soft sobs, muffled by the wooden door, escaped into the open space, tugging at his heart.

He knocked. Waited. At her shaky "Come in," he entered.

She sat on the bed, legs tucked up against her, but chastely hidden by the large folds of the bright white terry cloth robe.

She'd been crying. That was obvious from the redness of

her eyes and the soft flush on her cheeks marred by the remnants of her tears.

She swiped at her nose, sniffled, and said, "I was hoping I could wash my clothes."

He nodded and approached her slowly. "I can show you where the washer and dryer are once we get that new bandage on. I made some coffee. Thought you might like something to warm you up."

"Thanks. Coffee would be nice," she said and slipped off the bed.

He walked with her to the kitchen area, took some mugs from a cabinet, and pulled out a bottle of nondairy creamer. "It's all we have until we get our food delivery."

"That's okay. I like my coffee black," she said with a harsh laugh. "Funny what you remember, right?"

"It's a start," he said and stroked a hand down her back, offering comfort.

With a half-hearted smile, she echoed his comment. "It's a start."

The peal of the doorbell signaled that food had arrived. "Why don't you go back to your room for now."

She nodded and walked away, hands wrapped around the mug.

Mark opened the video app for the doorbell camera. It was Sergeant Millie Aviles, newly promoted from desk sergeant to working with their detectives.

He disarmed the alarm and opened the door with a smile. "Slow day?" he asked.

"Typical Sunday in Regina. Nice and quiet except for you, of course," she said as she pushed two bags of groceries at him. "I have another two in the car. Rhea went over-the-top to get you food and clothes."

He brought the bags to the kitchen table, and when Millie

returned, he took the other bags from her and also laid them on the table.

Millie looked around the room and, seeing that it was empty, said, "Jackson said we had a guest. Does she need anything besides food?"

At his puzzled look, she said, "Feminine products, Mark. If she does, I can swing by later with them."

"Thanks, Millie," he said, then walked her to the door and, once she was gone, reset the alarm.

Having heard the beeps of that, his "guest," as Millie had called her, returned to the kitchen area.

She gestured to the groceries on the table with her mug. "I can help you put those away."

"First the cut," he said, and pulled out a chair for her to sit.

As she did that, he went to the bathroom, located a first aid kit, and returned to the open-space area.

He sat opposite her and efficiently reapplied the butterfly bandage to the cut. Once he was done, he skimmed back a lock of hair that had fallen forward. It was silky beneath his fingers and slightly damp.

The touch, almost an intimate one, had him locking gazes with her until he abruptly pulled his hand away. "Sorry," he said and raised both hands in apology.

"It's okay. It felt nice. Like you…cared," she said and looked away, an embarrassed flush on her face. "I'm sorry. I just think it's been a while since anyone cared."

Which might explain why their search might not turn up a missing person report.

It made him sad to think that maybe no one cared.

"Let's see what we have for lunch. I'm hungry," he said, and as if to prove it, a loud growl erupted from his stomach, lightening the moment.

Together, they emptied the bags, which included deli meats and cheeses, rolls, beef and chicken for dinner, and several fruits and vegetables. Another bag held a bra, underwear, and a fleece sweat suit, as well as a change of clothes for him.

"Looks like we have everything…well, except feminine products. Sergeant Millie wants to know if you need any," he said, slightly uncomfortable with the discussion as he assumed most men would be.

"The bathroom is fully stocked," she said to alleviate his discomfort.

"Great. Let's make some lunch," he said.

"Let me change first," she said, then grabbed the clothes and rushed to her bedroom.

When she returned, he had placed the lunch items on a breakfast bar while she set the table.

In no time, they made sandwiches and sat kitty-corner at the table, silently eating.

"You like ham and cheese?" he said, hoping that the sandwich, much like the coffee, might elicit more memories.

"Who doesn't?" she said with a shrug and nibbled at her meal.

"My sister hates ham," he said and took a big bite.

She paused with her sandwich halfway to her mouth, as if suddenly recalling something, but then laid the sandwich down and shook her head. "It's so confusing. Just when I think I remember…"

He placed a hand on hers and gave a reassuring squeeze. "I'm sorry. I didn't mean to press. It's just that if you remember something, even the smallest memory, it might help keep you safe."

"I understand," she said and stared at the sandwich, obviously trying to piece something together, but then she just shook her head, obviously frustrated.

With another gentle squeeze, he said, "It'll come."

They finished the meal in silence. Cleaned up in much the same way.

"There are some books over there. Playing cards as well.

We have cable, so you can watch TV," he said, motioning to the built-in that held everything as well as a state-of-the-art entertainment system.

"TV sounds good. Mind-numbing. But won't that bother you?" she asked, peering around the open space, which, while nice, didn't offer much privacy.

"No, it won't. I'll just set up a laptop at the kitchen table," he said, and walked over to a drawer in the built-in that had a computer they kept there for anyone guarding the safe house.

EVEN THOUGH HE said it wouldn't bother him, she turned the volume down low so that he could work.

She hoped that he could help her figure out who she was and why she had been running away. Why she felt that, despite being in this safe house with a cop, she was in danger.

The sitcom was a popular one, and she was sure she had watched it before. It bothered her that she could remember such inane things while the most important memories eluded her.

But pressuring herself to remember was giving her a headache. Or maybe it was the blow to her head that might have caused her amnesia, according to the ER doctor. But what did he know? He was only a small-town doctor old enough to retire, unlike…

Unlike the big-city doctors she was used to.

But which big city? she thought, screwing her eyes shut to pull up that memory.

She failed to do so and just gave up. Forcing the issue wasn't helping, so she let herself get lost in the nonsensical jabberings of the thirtysomethings on-screen.

As she did so, the tap-tap-tap of his fingers on the keys filtered in, reassuring her once again. She was no longer alone. She had people who cared and would keep her safe.

Pulling a cozy throw from the end of the couch, she snuggled under it, and slowly, sleep claimed her until the beep-beep-beep of the alarm jerked her awake.

The police chief entered, a dour expression on his face. He closed the door, reset the alarm, and glanced in her direction before walking over and sitting on the edge of the couch.

"How are you feeling?" he asked, concern etched on his features.

"Better," she admitted, and it was the truth. The headache was gone, and while assorted aches and pains lingered in her body, she felt stronger.

"Please thank your wife for the groceries and clothes," she said, and plucked at the loose folds of the comfortable and warm sweatshirt.

"I will, and if you let me know your sizes, we'll pick up a few more items," Jackson said with a smile.

"Chief," Mark said as he took a seat opposite his boss, sandwiching her between them on the couch.

"I got an initial report from Crooked Pass Security, but I thought you should both hear what they've got to say," he said, and with a few taps on his screen, he sent a video call to the nearby television.

"You're getting good at that, Chief," Mark teased.

"I'm not a Luddite," Jackson parried, and a second later, the images of a man and woman, obviously siblings from their similar looks, popped onto the screen.

The woman was beautiful with dark, deep brown hair and intense blue eyes. Her brother had a head of thick tousled hair, and the same startling eyes, but a slightly bigger dimple in his chin.

"Let me introduce Sophie and Robbie Whitaker. My cousins and the founders of Crooked Pass Security. They are tech wizards, and if they can't work a problem, they know who can," Jackson said, familial pride ringing in his tone.

"Nice to meet you," the woman named Sophie said, her tone soothing and with no discernible trace of an accent.

And again, why did that matter to her, accent or not? she thought.

"Jackson asked us to find out what we could without sending up any flags," Robbie said, his tone a little more businesslike but still friendly.

"And?" she asked, cutting to the chase.

The siblings shared a look that sent a frisson of fear through her. "We spoofed our IP and created a fake ID so no one could track an AFIS search back to us. No hits, but that isn't surprising. Unless you committed a crime or needed to give your prints for a job, TSA PreCheck, or anything like that, we wouldn't get a hit," Robbie said, his tone one of forced calm.

"What aren't you saying?" Mark asked, beating her to the punch.

Another shared look came before Sophie faced the camera dead-on and said, "We couldn't get any kind of hit across any public places using our facial recognition software."

"No hits anywhere public? What about the federal databases?" Jackson pressed.

"We didn't want to push on the federal databases, just yet. Too risky, and besides, there's usually a lot of public info available," Robbie said.

"But you said you didn't get any hits," Mark said, just to be clear.

"No hits. Not anywhere on the internet or social media of any kind," Sophie replied.

Mark shook his head and said, "That seems unlikely."

"It does, considering that nearly eighty-four percent of people eighteen to twenty-nine have some kind of social media account," Robbie replied.

"What are you saying, Robbie?" Jackson said and dragged a hand through the longish strands of hair at the top of his head.

"That, for all purposes, your guest just doesn't exist."

Chapter Four

“What do you mean she doesn’t exist?” Mark asked since their “guest” was obviously sitting right beside him.

“Someone has scrubbed her from the internet, and the only one who normally does that is the government,” Sophie said, her tone slightly more sympathetic than her brother’s.

“The government?” their guest asked, fear and worry threaded in her voice.

“We talking spooks?” Jackson asked, a fair amount of fear also in his tone.

Sophie’s lips thinned into a tight slash, and she shook her head. “Spooks aren’t legally allowed to work domestically. I’d say either the FBI or Witness Protection.”

“If it’s either of those, that means I’m involved in something criminal, right?” their guest asked, straightening in her seat and leaning forward, awaiting a reply.

The CPS siblings shared a look and then nodded in unison.

“Yes, it does,” Robbie said.

“But it doesn’t mean you’re a criminal. They’d want to hide an innocent witness who’s testifying,” Sophie said.

The beautiful woman beside him clearly didn’t believe that as she sagged against the cushions of the sofa, worry clouding her features.

“Does that ring a bell?” he asked, wondering about the vibes he was getting from her.

Jackson shifted in his seat slightly to consider her as well. "Is there something you want to say?" he asked.

The woman shook her head vehemently, strands of her hair escaping the makeshift topknot. "I'm not a criminal. I can't be," she said, but it was almost as if she was trying to convince herself.

"Is that what you remember? Did you do something wrong?" Mark asked, sympathetic to her plight even though she might be someone he'd normally put behind bars.

She raised her hands to her temples, as if holding her head from shattering into pieces. "I don't know. There are so many confusing thoughts running through my head."

Mark met Jackson's gaze over her slouched figure. What he wanted was clear, so Mark comforted their guest. "Just relax and let things come when they're ready."

If she heard him, she didn't acknowledge it, so Jackson and he returned their attention to the CPS siblings.

"How much risk is there in searching the federal databases?" Jackson asked.

"There's a high risk it'll trip something, and they'll come knocking at our door," Robbie said.

Frustration flooded Mark's body, and he raked a hand through his hair. "And that would lead them to us, but we can't trust whoever is at the other end, even if they are the government."

"You're right. The fact that she was in those woods says there was an epic fail at their end," Sophie said, reinforcing his worries.

"Let's hold off on doing that. If she is part of some government operation and they had an epic fail, their first step is to try and fix the issue before anyone notices," Jackson said, and once again met Mark's gaze.

Mark nodded. "I agree. They'll try to hide their failure for as long as they can."

"Compartmentalizing. Solve this issue before having to move up the ladder to ask for help," Robbie said in agreement.

"If she's in witness protection—"

"Stop talking about me as if I'm not here," she said, shooting up into a sitting position, her blue-eyed gaze intense as it skipped from him to Jackson. Before they could say anything else, she said, "If I'm a witness, someone either messed up or wants me gone. I'm going with the latter."

"Or maybe you got cold feet about testifying and ran away," Mark said, earning an immediate guffaw from the woman.

She pointed to her skull and said, "The bump on the back of my head says otherwise."

It was hard to argue with that.

"Let's go with they want her gone," Jackson said and quickly added, "We keep her hidden until we know more."

"So that's a *no* to hitting the fed databases?" Sophie asked, brows raised in emphasis.

"It's a *no*. Try to find out what you can through other channels," Jackson said with a nod.

"Got it. We'll reach out to John and see what else he suggests," Robbie said, referring to their brother-in-law, John Wilson, a tech billionaire with even more resources and a powerful predictive outcome program.

"We also have the location pin that Mark sent. We'll have Diego and his K-9, Poppy, search the area to see if they can track her route. Do you have anything with her scent?" Sophie said.

"Yes, we have her clothes," Mark advised.

"Diego will come by the police station in the morning so Poppy can scent them," she said.

"We appreciate that," Mark and Jackson said, almost in unison, and a second later, the siblings ended the call.

A long, tense silence followed until the woman said, "I wish I could remember something. Anything."

Mark laid a reassuring hand on her shoulder. "It'll happen. I'm sure of it."

She wished she could be as sure. But her brain was just a jumble of thoughts, none of which seemed to make any sense.

She might be a witness to a crime.

Or worse, she might have committed a crime. Something about that was ringing a bell she didn't want rung.

I can't be a criminal, she told herself over and over.

I just can't, she thought, and met Mark's worried gaze.

"I know I wouldn't do anything wrong," she said, but even to her own ears it sounded as if she was trying to convince herself.

A gentle squeeze of his hand provided reassurance, but was it just an act?

Did he really care, or was he just playing whatever role he needed to so he could find out who wanted her gone?

That was one thing of which she was certain. Someone wanted her to disappear. She gingerly ran a hand across the big bump on her head.

He followed the motion, worry in his gaze, and then peered at his boss. "Unless you say otherwise, we stay here as long as necessary. Millie needs to know to keep this close to the vest. Same with the staff at the hospital."

"I'll let her know, although I'm sure Millie would know better than to blab about the safe house. Doc and the nurses can be trusted as well once I ask them to keep quiet," Jackson said.

"Unless it's fellow law enforcement doing the asking," Mark said, which had her searching her brain for any recollections about being with other cops. She'd been afraid of him after all.

The memories that came were of officers in uniform and a badge. A shiny silver badge with a gold circle at its center. Rays, like the sun, spread from the circle and were topped with…

She couldn't see what the emblem was or the words. Words that might have given her some clue.

"Don't push so hard," Mark said and rubbed her shoulder gently.

Forcing a smile, she said, "Easy for you to say."

He nodded and shifted his hand away as his boss rose and jerked his head to one side to ask Mark to walk with him.

Mark followed the police chief to the door, where they put their heads together and talked in tones so low she couldn't hear. But she could imagine what the discussion was about.

When the police chief sent a long, deliberate glance in her direction and then back to Mark, she sensed that he worried about leaving Mark and her together.

Did he see her as some kind of femme fatale who could distract his sergeant to escape?

She'd seen herself in the mirror after all. It wasn't wrong to admit that some might think she was beautiful.

And Mark was a handsome man.

She couldn't deny that, given any other circumstances, she would have found him attractive.

Was that going to be trouble?

Jackson clapped his sergeant on the back, shot her another inquiring look, and then walked out.

Mark quickly reset the alarm and leaned against the door. Glancing her way, he said, "Looks like it's the two of us for now. I'm going to review the materials I have and see what else I can find. Why don't you get some rest."

She felt like rest was the last thing she needed. What she needed was to know who she was and why she was in this predicament.

But the memories were a jumble, and pushing too hard did make her head hurt.

Maybe rest, especially mindless rest in front of the television, would help break open whatever dam was holding back her memories.

"I'm going to lie on the couch and relax. Maybe that'll help."

Mark watched her get comfy on the sofa and flip on the television again.

He hoped that the amnesia was only temporary and that something would trigger the memories they needed to find out why someone had attacked and imprisoned her. But amnesia was a tricky thing. Uncertain, and they couldn't wait for her memory to return since she was clearly in danger.

He poured himself a fresh cup of coffee, added lots of cream and sugar, and returned to the laptop to skim through the assorted missing persons reports in the area.

It took over an hour of peering at the faces of so many young people, mostly women of various races, to confirm his guest wasn't one of them. If she wasn't a missing person, had she either voluntarily run or escaped from a Witness Protection program?

But if she was a witness, what had been her role in the crime? Innocent bystander or active participant?

Does it matter? the little voice in his head asked. Whether a bystander or participant, he needed to protect her.

Which meant that he, along with Jackson, his fellow officers, and Crooked Pass Security, had to do what they could until they knew why she was in danger.

He'd keep searching, and in the morning, CPS Agent Diego Rodriguez would use his K-9, Poppy, to search the woods from the spot where Mark had dropped a pin.

Mark was familiar with that area, which had several hiking trails as well as homes near the ski runs higher up on the mountainside. Many were vacation homes, but there were also full-time residents.

If Witness Protection had stowed her nearby, he bet that it would be in one of the vacation homes since it was too late for skiing and too early to take advantage of the lake activities in Regina.

He could review maps of the area from other recent investigations. But as he took a quick look at his watch, he decided to take a break and start dinner.

Rhea had sent them all the ingredients they needed for a hearty stew, and it would hit the spot after the morning chill and the distressing revelations of the day. A filling bowl of comfort food might even help with her memories. They said that the taste and smell of food could elicit memories of not just the food, but also of the places and people connected to it.

He closed the laptop and stood, and when he did so, she peered in his direction.

Jerking a thumb toward the kitchen, he said, "I was going to get dinner going."

"Can I help?" she said and rose even before he answered.

"Sure. That would be great. I was going to make stew," he said, thinking that maybe helping prep the meal might also trigger some kind of recollection.

"Stew sounds good," she said, then joined him at the counter and patiently waited as he pulled beef cubes, carrots, and celery from the fridge.

"Want to peel the carrots?" he asked, and at her nod, he handed her the bag and rummaged in the drawers until he found a peeler and passed it to her.

She got to work, and he went to where he had earlier stowed the potatoes and onions. He took some potatoes over to her and quickly sliced up some onions and chopped some celery.

Once he was done with that, he returned to the cabinets to pull out a large stockpot.

He was about to sauté the beef when he noticed that she had stopped, set down the peeler, and was staring at her hands, clearly puzzled by something.

"Do you remember something?"

Chapter Five

The long curl of carrot peel dropped to the counter and roused a memory. A confusing one that kept her from answering his question.

He swept a gentle hand down her back and turned slightly, coming into her line of sight. Almost imploring her to answer.

"I saw…two pairs of hands. Identical hands. Peeling carrots."

"Your mom and you?" he asked, his tone cautious and caring.

She shook her head. "No, they were small hands."

Meeting his gaze, she said, "It was like I was having double vision. I don't get it."

He gave a sympathetic nod. "Concussions can cause double vision."

"Maybe," she said, but didn't quite believe it. The vision, the memory, had been way too clear, but also way too confusing.

"I like lots of carrots in my stew. How about you?" she asked, since that was something else that had come to her as she peeled.

"I love carrots. Turnips, too, but we only have potatoes," he said as he worked on browning the meat. Seemingly satisfied, he scooped up some onions he had sliced and tossed them in the pot.

He worked confidently, and she could tell that he was someone who regularly cooked. He'd handled finding her confidently as well, and she wondered if there was anything that fazed the young cop.

Not that he was that much younger than her. If anything,

they were about the same age, only she was feeling old. Heavy from the weight of not knowing who she was and why someone might want to hurt her.

She finished prepping the last few carrots. As she worked, Jackson's and Mark's earlier words about her being in Witness Protection came back to her.

Am I an innocent witness or a criminal? she wondered with a long, slow stroke of the peeler.

Innocent was the immediate reply from the little voice in her head, and as much as she wanted to believe that, her gut warned that might not be the case.

She shoved that feeling aside and peeled more vigorously, rinsed the carrots, and was about to slice them, but stopped and asked, "Chunky or thin?"

He glanced up from stirring the meat and onions and smiled. "Chunky? You okay with that?"

His smile loosened the anxious knot in her gut, and she smiled back and nodded. "I like chunky, too."

It was weird she could remember those little details, but not more. It was like there was a dam in her brain that had a hole where only small bits could leak out while the big memories stayed trapped behind the dam.

In no time, the stew was simmering on the stove. "We'll add the potatoes later. Don't want them to get mushy," he said, his tone earnest.

"No mushy potatoes," she said with a laugh, surprised she could find humor in anything considering her situation.

Mark chuckled and shook his head. "I take cooking way too seriously."

"Surprising for a single guy," she said, but then immediately added, "Sorry. It's wrong to assume you're single."

Mark held his hands up in surrender. "Guilty as charged. Single, but I don't live on takeout or DoorDash. My mom taught all her boys the basics."

"That's great. My mom…" she began, but then the memory that had been there dissipated like morning fog beneath the sun.

Tears came to her eyes. "I almost had something and then…"

He cupped her cheek and offered a sympathetic smile. "It'll happen."

"What if it doesn't? What if I can never remember my mother, or father, or if I have any siblings? Worse, whether I'm a criminal?" she choked out, throat tight with emotion.

"Have you ever heard the term *tabula rasa*?" he asked and stroked his thumb across her cheek to brush away a tear.

She searched her brain, but came up empty. Again. "No, I haven't."

"Some believe that we're born with a blank slate. That there's nothing there until we have experiences to fill that slate. Others think we already have memories and traits here," he said, and splayed a hand directly over his heart.

She mimicked his motion and pressed the center of her chest, wishing she could feel something. Anything, even if it was something painful.

Instead, she felt hollow. Empty. As if that slate was empty, maybe forever.

She screwed her eyes shut against a fresh wave of pain and in a strangled voice said, "I need a moment."

SHE RACED OFF to her bedroom and slammed the door shut.

Not even the thick wooden door could hide the sound of her sobs, but Mark didn't interfere with her crying. She struck him as someone with a spine of steel, but that didn't mean she couldn't have her moments.

Especially considering her situation.

And the only way to make things better was to find out exactly what that situation was.

He did a quick stir of the stew and then returned to the

kitchen table, intent on finding anything that might help their investigation.

Opening his laptop, he pulled up LIDAR images from a few years back and an investigation into the disappearance of Rhea's twin sister. Jackson had been the detective in charge of that case, and Diego and his K-9 had also assisted in finding her missing twin. The images had pinpointed several structures in the area, but as he deepened his review, he realized that the locale covered by the LIDAR survey was too far over on the mountain from the trail.

He was about to review another set of images when the bedroom door opened and she strolled out, face pale. As their gazes locked, she wrung her hands together in a nervous gesture.

"Would you mind checking on the stew?" he said, hoping that the simple task might restore some level of calm, maybe even normalcy in what was otherwise a very abnormal situation.

"Sure," she said and forced a smile.

From the corner of his eye, he saw her stir and check the meat. "Beef's still tough. It may be another hour or so before we can put in the potatoes."

"Thanks for checking," he said, and she immediately blurted out, "I can keep an eye on it so you can work."

He nodded and smiled. "That would be great."

With a dip of her head, she did another stir and then returned to the living room, where she huddled on the couch, a light throw tossed over her legs. A second later, the sounds of a classic sitcom filled the air.

Good. Rest and something hopefully familiar might help her in multiple ways. A moment of peace, for one. Possibly rousing memories, for another.

Returning to work, he examined a set of satellite images that showed several structures and homes on the mountain. Zooming in to view the vicinity in and around the hiking trail where he had found her, he tried to piece together which of the buildings were in the general direction from which she might have escaped.

He did not doubt that she had escaped.

But if she had been in the care of Witness Protection, there had been an epic fail, as Sophie had said. Someone had taken her and imprisoned her. He didn't know whether it was an outsider or someone within the program. What worried him was that his gut was saying it was an inside job.

He identified several structures where she might have been held. All were at least a mile or more from the hiking trail, which only raised his estimation of her spine of steel.

It wouldn't have been easy to go that distance through the underbrush and forest separating the assorted buildings from the hiking trail.

More than half an hour had passed during his review, and she must have realized that as well since she rose and went to check on their dinner. She stirred, then spooned up a piece of the meat, which she pinched with her fingers. "Just a little bit more. I'll prep the potatoes and get them in," she said, and tossed a glance in his direction over her shoulder.

"Sounds great. I'm getting a little hungry," he said, and in response, his stomach grumbled noisily.

"If I remember, Rhea—that was her name, right?" she asked, eyes narrowed in question.

"Yes, Rhea. Jax's wife," he answered.

"She brought some take-and-bake rolls, I think," she said and popped open the freezer. With a satisfied "ah," she pulled out.the bag and held it up. "Perfect for the stew."

His stomach sounded even louder with the thought of dunking yeasty bread into the tasty gravy. "It is. Do you need help with anything?" he asked, not wanting to push her or seem chauvinistic by expecting her to do the dinner chores. He didn't normally ask others to do, he just did, so he was slightly uncomfortable with this new dynamic.

"I'm good. I was going to make a salad, if you'd like," she said.

"I'd like. Thanks," he said and returned to work while she toiled in the kitchen, cleaning and cutting the potatoes. Adding them to the stew, and after, turning her attention to the take-and-bake rolls and a salad.

Mark had turned his attention to printing out the images he had identified that might be of help, and once he was done, he texted Jackson.

Got some info for Diego. A map of the area would be great. Do we have one at the station?

There was a long delay before the police chief responded.

We do. Will bring over before I head home for dinner.

Dinner, he repeated silently, and decided it was time he made another contribution to their meal.

He closed the laptop, laid it on a nearby side table, and set out place mats, glasses, napkins, and cutlery.

Walking over to where she was busily chopping lettuce, he was about to lay a hand on the small of her back, but jerked his hand away. It would be too intimate a gesture for virtual strangers, even though being forced into proximity with her was creating a too-intimate feel.

While she worked on the salad, he checked the stew, and as he did so, the enticing aromas of the baking bread and hearty meal teased his nostrils. "Everything smells great."

"I've been working hard all day," she teased with a laugh.

"Wait a second. I think I helped a little," he said, humor ringing in his tone.

She raised her hand and inched together her thumb and forefinger. "A little would be right," she said, her blue-eyed gaze bright. It had lost some of its earlier sadness and worry.

Determined to keep that mood in the hopes it would help with her recovery, he didn't push. He went to the fridge and pulled out butter for the rolls and also some bottles of iced tea and pop that he placed on the table.

He returned to the stove and checked on the stew, piercing the potatoes with a fork. Tender, he thought. Bending, he turned on the oven light and peered at the rolls. Still a little pale.

"Not long. Just a few more minutes," he said and faced her.

"Great. I can't believe it, but I'm hungry," she said and laid a hand against her belly.

"Me, too. Why don't you sit, and I'll serve?" he offered.

"I'd like that. Thank you," she said, then grabbed the salad and sat at the head of the table.

Interesting, he thought. Her action told him that she was used to being in some kind of leadership position since the person in that seat traditionally communicated that they were the one with the power.

To help gain her trust, he'd make a point to sit next to her to create a sense of togetherness rather than opposite her, which might communicate defensiveness.

He ladled out healthy portions of stew, making sure that they both got a lion's share of the carrots they both seemed to love.

He served her first and then placed his bowl at his spot. After, he took out the rolls, which had baked to golden deliciousness. He dumped them into a basket and placed it next to the salad before sitting adjacent to her.

"Thank you," she said and smiled. It reached into her brilliant blue eyes, pleasing him that she was seemingly comfortable with him, given all that had happened to her.

He had intended to keep the dinner conversation neutral, but hunger took over, making it a relatively silent meal punctuated by satisfied sighs and compliments on how well the meal had turned out.

"I don't remember having such a tasty meal in a long time," he said, and wanted to bite his tongue as her earlier peacefulness fled.

"I just don't remember," she said sadly.

He was about to apologize when the sound of the beep-beep-beep of the alarm warned that someone was entering.

"Just Jax," he said as she jumped slightly in her chair until the police chief came in and locked the door behind him.

THE SOUND OF the alarm had caused a scare that made her heart race, but she sucked in a breath to control it at the sight of the police chief as he entered.

Since Mark and he had business to discuss, she said, "I'll clean up so you can get back to work."

She busied herself with clearing the table, loading the dishwasher, and putting away the remainder of the stew, which would be enough for another dinner. That is, if she was still the guest of the Regina Police Department for any length of time.

Judging by how earnestly the two men were chatting, their goal was to get her somewhere else—preferably home—as soon as possible.

But first and foremost, they needed to know why someone wanted her gone. Then and only then would going home be a realistic option.

Almost on cue, the two men glanced her way, and Mark said, "I've located some buildings in the area and hope you'll take a look at them. See if anything seems familiar."

"Sure," she said, filled with both dread and hope that memory would flood back.

With a nod, Mark walked to a printer at the far side of the living room built-in, while Jackson gestured with his hand for her to join them at the kitchen table.

She did, letting Jackson sit at the head of the table while she sat beside him. Mark returned a second later with a small sheaf of papers and took a spot beside her. Being surrounded by the men brought a new sense of comfort in comparison with the fear that had earlier dominated every cell of her body.

Progress, she thought, until Mark spread out the half a dozen or so photos on the tabletop.

She peered at them for long minutes, scrutinizing them intently. There were a few small cabins like the kind you might use as a weekend retreat. The other homes were of varying sizes, from modest to one immense contemporary home of glass and sharp angles.

Dangerous angles swept into her brain, but she pushed that thought aside and lifted the photo of one of the cabins. She examined it carefully before laying it down and scooping up the next photo.

The men remained silent as she repeated the process for each and every photo, leaving that worrisome contemporary to the very end.

Her hand shook as she reached for the photo, as if even touching it might cause harm.

Both Jackson and Mark noticed her hesitation.

"Does that one look familiar?" the chief asked.

She sucked in a deep breath, held it to tamp down the fear roiling her gut, and then blurted out, "Maybe. There's just something…menacing about it. The hard glass. Sharp angles."

A memory slammed into her of clinging to a cold, hard metal surface like you might find on a glass window.

"I was hanging from a window like one of those," she said, and pointed to the contemporary home. But then she shook her head and said, "But I can't say for sure if it was this house."

"It's a start," Mark said and offered encouragement with a reassuring stroke of his hand along her arm.

Two steps forward and one step back, she thought.

She met his gaze, sympathetic as always. "Are there other homes like this in the area?"

He nodded. "Yes, I just picked those closest to where I found you. I can widen the search."

With a dip of her head, she said, "I remember trudging through the woods for a while. I think it was dark when I started."

Another memory slammed into her then, making her touch the butterfly bandage on her forehead. "I tripped and fell during the walk because I couldn't see where I was going. That's when I hit my head on a stump or something."

Chapter Six

"That's great," Mark said, relieved that she was finally starting to recall what had happened to her.

With another reassuring stroke of his hand along her arm, he said, "Hopefully, you'll recognize something else from the new images I find."

"Hopefully," she said, and for the first time, he detected a hint of optimism in her tone.

"If you don't mind giving me that photo, we'll run a property search to see who owns it and if they live there or rent it out," Jackson said and held his hand out for the paper.

Since she didn't reach for it, a clue that she was still uneasy about that property, Mark handed the photo to his boss.

"This may be our first break, or it may be nothing," Jackson said as he took a last look at the image before standing. "But I'll work on this in the meantime and wait to see what else you find."

"I'll send anything relevant," Mark said and escorted Jackson to the front door, the woman trailing behind them, but she stayed several feet from the door, as if getting too close presented risk.

Had she been grabbed when she answered her door? Mark wondered, thinking it might explain that reticence.

Jackson paused and peered at the woman. "My wife, Rhea, said she'd get you some other clothes and shoes if you can let us know your sizes."

The woman immediately rattled off, "Size nine shoe. Size six jeans. Large for tops."

Jackson smiled and nodded, seemingly pleased by a quick response that said memory was maybe returning. "Good. I'll bring some other things tomorrow."

He exited, and Mark closed the door and reset the alarm.

"I'll work on investigating the other buildings soon, but first, I have to feed Rocky and let him get some exercise."

She glanced at the large cane corso, who lifted his massive black head as if realizing they were talking about him.

"He must eat a lot. He's a big boy," she said as Mark did some kind of hand command, and the large dog ambled over.

Mark stroked Rocky's head and then rubbed just behind his ears. "He's just a big baby. But don't underestimate what a great guard dog he is."

She eyeballed the "big baby" and thought once again that just his sheer size would discourage anyone from attacking. "Is he bred for that?"

"He is. Cane corsos are Italian mastiffs and used primarily for guarding and companionship. But they also were once used for herding cattle and hunting game, so Diego and I thought Rocky would be a good choice for the new division," Mark explained.

"Sounds like it," she said, and when Mark gave Rocky another hand command, the dog followed him into the kitchen area. Mark grabbed some bowls from a cabinet and filled one with kibble and the other with water.

The dog immediately lapped up some water and then attacked the food, emptying the bowl with just a few quick bites.

When he was done, he sat back on his haunches and looked at Mark as if asking, "Is that all there is?"

Mark laughed, rubbed the dog's head, and said, "Time for some fun."

The dog barked and raced toward the front door, but Mark

called him back and led him toward a rear sliding glass door to one side of the kitchen.

There was an alarm keypad there as well, so he disarmed it and opened the door. Rocky immediately raced out.

Mark looked at her. "Want to come with?"

Fear filled her at the thought of being outdoors again. She'd had her share of it earlier. She shook her head, and Mark didn't try to dissuade her, which she appreciated. She'd had too much of people trying to control her…

She did a little jump, wondering where that memory had come from.

"You okay?" Mark asked, eyes narrowed as he scrutinized her.

She nodded. "I just remembered something, but I'm not sure what it means."

"Okay," he said with a dip of his head, but he didn't press. Again, a point in his favor.

He reset the alarm, exited, and slid the door closed behind him.

Even though she didn't want to go outside, she was interested in learning more about Mark and Rocky.

She leaned against the wall, crossed her arms, and watched as man and beast—and he was quite a large beast—played in the yard. Mark had located a big stick that he tossed, and Rocky chased after it before returning it.

When both man and dog seemingly tired of that, Mark gave a hand command to the dog, which had Rocky running and barking playfully as Mark did circles around the small yard. Finally tired, Mark stopped, hands on his hips, as he drew in rough breaths from his exertions.

As he did so, his gaze connected with hers, and he shot her a dimpled smile.

The dimples made her heart stop and her stomach do a little jump. She laid a hand over her midsection to calm the unwanted reaction.

Attraction to the handsome cop was the last thing she needed at the moment.

Because of that, she rushed away from the door, giving herself distance from any possible temptation.

MARK CAUGHT THE slight look of dismay on her face before she raced away from the sliding door.

He narrowed his gaze, puzzled by her reaction.

Rocky nudged his hand with his large head and sat beside him.

Mark looked down at him, and the dog also seemed slightly puzzled.

He chalked it up to the very emotional day they'd had. Even he found it hard to believe how much had happened in just a few hours. From finding her on the trail to all the investigations they'd already done, which had created more questions than answers.

He couldn't see her as a criminal.

Not that it wasn't possible, but he considered himself a pretty good judge of character, and his radar wasn't going off around her.

With a heavy sigh, he figured it was as good a time as any to go back to work. Especially since dusk had arrived and it would be dark soon. He would have to do a patrol around the house, but later, when it was full dark, so as not to attract attention from the neighbors.

Entering the home, the beep-beep-beep of the alarm and the sound of the television welcomed him back. Once Rocky had sidled past him, he closed the door and reset the alarm. Rocky ambled back to his spot in the living room and lay down.

Mark retrieved the laptop and sat at the kitchen table. He expanded the area he'd already covered and zoomed in to search for homes that looked like the one that had caused a reaction in their guest.

Repeatedly, he scoured the drone and satellite images, magnifying them to locate anything worthwhile.

He finally found a similar home that was on the right longitude to where he'd found her. But it was nearly four miles away, and the forest between the home and the trail was heavily wooded. There was also some pretty deep underbrush for large portions of the way.

Looking in her direction, where she snuggled into a corner of the couch, appearing delicate, it occurred to him once again that she had a spine of steel. It hadn't been an easy trek she'd made after escaping. That very early morning escape would jibe with how long it might take to go from the house to the trail, given the physical conditions of the mountainside.

He switched to one of the real estate programs in the hope they'd have photos of the house from either a prior or current sale, or even a rental.

No entry on any real estate site, even though it was a fairly substantial home.

No street view. Was that unusual? he wondered.

To confirm that, he located a few nearby homes, and lo and behold, there were street views, even of the most remote home farther up on the mountain.

Had the real estate entries and street views been scrubbed, much like her existence had disappeared?

Pulling up a map, he superimposed the satellite images with a street map and managed to get a rough street address. He sent that info to Jackson and copied Robbie and Sophie at Crooked Pass Security, asking them if they could find details on the home.

Both confirmed they would work on it despite the late hour.

He'd been so involved with the search, he hadn't realized that it was almost ten. Well past time for another patrol and letting Rocky relieve himself.

The chair creaked as he rose, rousing the woman, who must have drifted off.

"I'm doing a quick patrol around the house. I won't be long."

She gestured toward the bedrooms. "I'm going to go to bed."

"Have an easy night," he said, hoping today's rest and a good night's sleep might help her recover some of the buried truths in her brain.

She forced a smile that didn't reach those crystalline blue eyes and dipped her head. "Good night and thank you. I don't know what would have happened if you hadn't been there."

He thought about it for a quick second. "Somehow, I think you would have figured out."

The smile widened and finally filled that beautiful gaze with what might be joy. With a nod, she said, "Yeah. I think so, too."

With that, she hurried to the bedroom, and he whistled softly to Rocky. The dog shot to his feet and loped over, eager for the activity.

This assignment was going to test the canine, who needed a lot of activity.

It's going to test you as well, the little voice in his head warned. *Both as a K-9 officer and a man.*

Ignoring that annoying voice, he harnessed Rocky and rushed off for that final night patrol. As he exited onto the front porch, he caught sight of one of Regina's police cruisers doing a slow roll down the block.

Not unusual. Nightly patrols were a routine thing in Regina. But he suspected Jackson had instructed the officers to add extra patrols in and around the safe house area and to be discreet about it.

Because of that, he only dipped his head to acknowledge their passing, did a leisurely walk down to the curb, and then to the backyard gate.

He opened the gate, secured it, and slipped the leash off Rocky so he could run free and relieve himself. Rocky happily did a couple of laps around the backyard, sniffing and scenting the area until he found an acceptable spot and let nature take its course.

Mark strolled over and cleaned up. After, he vigorously rubbed the cane corso's body, something that he'd learned the dog enjoyed.

Rocky rewarded him with a sloppy kiss.

Laughing, Mark wiped away the worst of it, then massaged Rocky again before issuing a hand command for the dog to follow him back into the house.

Once the alarm was reset, Mark ambled over to the couch to watch some television because he was too wired to sleep. Rocky joined him, lying at his feet in the narrow space between the couch and the coffee table.

Flipping on the television, he turned the volume down and activated the closed captions so as not to disturb her, and also so he could hear anything out of the ordinary going on.

Settling into the cushions, he drew in a deep breath to relax.

A big mistake.

A fresh, very feminine fragrance filled his nostrils since he was in the spot she'd been occupying for most of the day and evening.

Marshaling control, he surfed through the various channels, searching for mindless entertainment to wipe his brain clean. Jackson had taught him that you needed to be fresh and clear-headed when on the job.

He hurried past the true crime and investigation programs. They were too close to his real life.

Baking was not his jam, but he loved to cook and set his attention on a show on quick weeknight meals. Just the thing he needed with his busy schedule. Even though being a cop in Regina was a great gig, working with Diego on training

Rocky, Diego's canine, Poppy, and a few other pups took up a good amount of his time. They hoped to assign the dogs they trained to other Regina police officers and Crooked Pass Security agents.

The show did as he hoped.

The tension of the day slowly fled, and he relaxed, sinking into the cushions. Slightly drowsy until he heard a sharp, almost painful cry from her bedroom.

A second later, a shrill, bloodcurdling scream pierced the quiet of the night and was followed by a loud crash.

Mark bolted to his feet and raced toward her bedroom, Rocky chasing after him.

Chapter Seven

She shot up in bed, screaming, and thrashed out, knocking a lamp off the nearby bedside table.

Breathing heavily, she wrapped her arms around herself and tried to get control.

As her eyes adjusted to the dark, she remembered that she was no longer captive. She was safe here. *Safe*, she told herself over and over.

The door burst open, and light spilled into the room.

The shadow of a man, gun drawn, and an immense dog filled the space a second before the ceiling light snapped on.

"I'm okay," she said shakily and met his gaze, trying to steady hers to convince him that there was no present danger.

He hesitated, did a slow look around the room, and then finally holstered his gun. With a softly voiced command, the dog sat just outside her door.

He approached, sympathy in his gaze, and when he reached her, he picked up the lamp and then sat on the edge of the bed.

"Are you sure you're okay?" he asked, concern etched onto his features.

"I had a nightmare," she admitted as she tried to make sense of the kaleidoscope of images from her tortured slumber. Slowly, the pieces came together, and she shared them.

Eyes narrowed as she held on to the memories, she said, "I remember a house. Like the one you showed me earlier."

He nodded and said, "Could you identify it if we showed you a photo?"

She bobbed her head up and down forcefully. "Yes, I think I could."

"Do you remember anything else?"

She closed her eyes and thinned her lips as she reached for the images. They came more easily, and she met his sharp, green-eyed gaze. "A man. Older."

"Was he the one holding you captive?" he asked, his eyes skipping over her face, waiting for her reaction.

She shrugged, uncertain. "He scared me, but I'm not sure."

"You screamed. Was it because you were scared?" he asked and did a reassuring stroke of his hand down her arm, urging her to release the death grip she had on herself.

Shaking her head, she said, "I think I screamed because I fell down a cliff of some kind, and it was dark, and I didn't know what would happen. If I would die."

Her body shook, almost involuntarily, as she relived that moment again.

As he had before, he offered support with a gentle swipe of his hand down to hers. He took it into his hand and said, "You're safe now."

"For how long?" she shot back quickly, certain that whoever had taken her wouldn't be content to have her running free.

His face hardened, growing stony. Those lips capable of that dimpled, easygoing smile became a harsh slash across his face. "As long as I draw breath," he said with such conviction that she had no doubt he meant it.

That scared her as much as the thought of being taken again. She cradled the strong line of his jaw and ran a thumb across those mobile lips.

"I won't let it come to that. I'd rather they take me than that," she vowed and hoped she could keep that promise.

His lips softened into a hesitant smile. "Let's promise each other that it won't happen."

She nodded and expelled a rough breath. "I promise."

"Good," he said and pushed to his feet. "Try to get some rest."

"You, too," she said as she snuggled back under the covers, but when he neared the door, she popped back up.

"Can you leave the door open and the light on?"

"SURE. I'LL BE RIGHT out there," he said and jerked a thumb in the direction of the couch.

Not the best place to sleep, but he'd had worse when camping or on an assignment.

"Or you could stay close. Just in case," she said and snuck a quick peek at the space beside her in the queen-size bed.

Sucking in a deep breath, he rocked back and forth on his heels and said, "I'm not sure that's such a good idea."

"O-o-h," she said and eyeballed him intently. "You're probably right."

With a strangled cough, he said, "Sleep tight," and closed the door halfway so light could spill in to reassure her. For good measure, he instructed Rocky to guard the door.

"*Pass auf*," he said, and the dog lay across her door.

Hoping that would be enough to calm her fears and let her rest, he hurried to the couch to get a much-needed breather.

The one cooking show had finished, but luckily, they were running a marathon.

Snuggling down into the sofa cushions, her fragrance wrapped around him. Torturous, but also calming. It was a fresh, floral scent reminiscent of the meadow that Rocky and he had hiked earlier that day before…

Before his life had possibly changed forever.

He didn't know why he thought that, but he did.

That feeling chased him into an uneasy sleep until a sharp trill of his cell phone warned that he had a message.

Jackson, he realized after a bleary-eyed peek at his phone.

CPS has news. Will be over in an hour for a meeting with Sophie and Robbie.

An hour. He peered at the time. Barely seven. An early start to the day, but that was the nature of the beast when you were a cop.

Time enough to start the coffee, take a shower, and get a fresh change of clothes. Hopefully, he'd feel human after that trio.

But first, taking care of Rocky.

He went to the sliding door, disarmed the alarm, and opened it so his partner could get some fresh air and do his duty. Chill air swept in, reminding him that winter was holding on despite it being late spring.

After closing the door, he was headed to the kitchen when she stepped out into the common area.

"Good morning. You're up early," she said.

"Good morning. Jackson will be by in an hour for a meeting with CPS," he said. "You're up early, too," he added.

With a shrug, she said, "I'm an early riser."

The comment seemed to surprise her, as so many did. Each revealed something while the big pieces remained elusive.

She jerked an elegant hand in the direction of the kitchen. "I can make the coffee. I assume you want a shower and to change," she said with a cute wrinkle of her nose.

He sniffed. "I didn't realize I was that aromatic."

She waved her hands in apology. "You're not. You smell great. It's just that—"

He snared her hands to stop her. "Just kidding. I won't be

long," he said, then hurried to the sliding door to let Rocky back in, set the alarm, and instructed the dog to guard the area.

HOT COLOR FILLED her face as he walked away, and she turned her attention to making breakfast so they could eat before the meeting with Crooked Pass Security.

She hoped that they'd have info that would help her remember more and figure out who might want to hurt her.

The everyday routine of coffee, making toast, and cooking the eggs brought unexpected calm. Maybe because the actions represented normal life when everything else was anything but that.

Her movements in the kitchen were sure, as if it were something she regularly did.

As soon as enough coffee had dripped out, she poured a cup and almost greedily gulped it down. The heat slipped down her throat, warming her.

The metallic pop of the toaster warned that it needed attention. She plucked the toast out and prepped more. While the second pair toasted, she buttered the first slices, mouth watering at the thought of eating.

Overhead, the sibilant sound of water in the pipes stopped. He'd be ready for breakfast soon.

She cracked several eggs into a bowl, added some milk, and scrambled them. She had never been good at making fried eggs.

Another simple thing to remember, but this time, as she closed her eyes, the memory expanded, bringing a brief look of an older woman and her cooking. Only something struck her as not quite right.

How could she be seeing herself with the woman as if she were an outsider watching the scene? she wondered.

The snick of his door opening ripped her from the memory and caused her body to do a little jump, as if she was dropping back into it after an out-of-body experience.

Mark narrowed his gaze as he noticed. "Everything okay?"

She nodded, even if it wasn't. But she didn't quite know how to describe what had just happened and needed time to process it.

"I'm okay. Can I make the eggs? I'd hate for them to get cold if you're not ready," she said, and heard an echo of another voice as she did so. That older woman. Her mother, she thought.

"Yes. I'll just be a few minutes. I need to feed Rocky," he said.

Mark prepped Rocky's morning food and a large bowl of water. As the dog finished, Mark massaged the immense dog's sides and head, earning kisses and pulling a smile and laughter from the police officer.

It made her smile and almost forget why she was here with the cop and his dog.

She did a few more stirs of the eggs and, satisfied they were done, scooped them onto plates and added the buttered toast while Mark made his coffee.

He held up the pot and asked, "Do you need a refill?"

"Not yet," she said and took their plates over to the table, where they sat and ate in comfortable silence.

"Delicious," he said as he forked up the last of the eggs.

"Thanks. Not all that hard to do," she said and popped the last bit of toast into her mouth.

"You haven't met my sister. She can't even make toast," he said with a laugh, then stood and grabbed their plates. "You cook, I clean."

But he had no sooner reached the sink when the sound of a key in the lock had them both peering at the front door.

Jackson entered a second later, carrying a big bag that appeared to be filled with clothes.

After resecuring the door, he walked over and held out the bag to her. "Rhea hopes you like her selections."

"Thank you, and please thank her," she said and took the bag from him.

Jackson shot a quick look at his watch. "Almost time. Do you mind if I grab a cup?" he said and gestured toward the coffeemaker.

She held her hand out in invitation. "Help yourself. Let me put these away."

"I'll finish cleaning so we can start the meeting," Mark said, and with a nod, she walked to her bedroom.

MARK QUICKLY CLEANED while Jackson leaned on the counter beside him.

"Anything?" his boss asked with an arch of a sandy-colored brow.

Mark shrugged. "She had a nightmare. Remembers falling after she escaped. She thinks she might be able to ID the building where she had been kept. Also remembers an older man, but she's not sure he's the one who imprisoned her."

With a bobble of his head and a sip of his coffee, Jackson said, "It's a start."

A slow one, Mark thought, but he was still grateful for even that.

He followed Jackson to the living room, where his boss snapped on the television and started the video feed for the meeting. Seconds later, Robbie and Sophie joined.

"Good morning. I hope you didn't work too late," Jackson said to his cousins.

"Not too late," Robbie said with an easy smile.

The woman entered the living room, dressed in a deep blue flowing blouse and stylish jeans instead of the loose sweats she'd been wearing earlier.

Rhea had done a nice job, Mark thought as he peered at her. She looked wonderful in a girl-next-door kind of way.

She seemed uncomfortable with his scrutiny as she ran her

hands down the soft fabric of the blouse. "Not my usual style, but pretty."

It struck him again that she could remember some things but not others. It almost made him wonder if she was intentionally hiding the other big reveals. She could be a criminal after all, that little voice in his head warned, while his gut fought that idea.

"Good morning," she said, and sat beside him on the couch.

The techies echoed the greeting, but then Sophie immediately launched into the meeting.

"You gave us some good info last night, Mark," she said and displayed the images and other info he had gleaned from his research.

"We tried to find more on that location, but hit the same roadblocks that you did. Someone clearly wiped that home's info from almost all databases," Robbie said.

"*Almost* all. Do I gather you found it somewhere?" Jackson pressed.

"Yes, and no," Sophie said and then displayed what looked like architectural plans.

"We used the approximate address for the location and searched that town's zoning approvals and building permits. We found the plans that had been filed and approved as well as the permits and inspections," she added.

"So someone scrubbed the info, but didn't eliminate evidence there," Mark said, just to make sure he was understanding.

"Yes, they didn't think to dig through routine paperwork. Another possible failure, although to be fair, not many would do as deep a dive as we would," Robbie said and hesitated before plowing on with their report.

"We took those plans as well as the topographical info from the maps you sent. Applying our AI software and Wilson's predictive program, we recreated what the home and surrounding landscape would look like."

That hesitation came again, and the siblings shared a look before Sophie said, "Are you ready to see it?"

He had no doubt she was referring to their guest, who was nervously rubbing her palms across her thighs.

He laid a reassuring hand on her shoulder, leaned close, and in soft tones said, "Do you want to see it?"

She pulled in a deep breath and held it before expelling a sibilant "Yes-s-s-s."

Chapter Eight

Her body trembled in a tangled mix of fear and anticipation as she waited for the big reveal.

When the image appeared a second later, her heart hiccuped in her chest, and all breath escaped her in a surprised, "No."

"No?" Mark and Jackson asked, almost in unison.

She shook her head and said, "Sorry, yes. That's the home. I meant no way were you able to get that from what you had."

"The AI and predictive programs used info on building materials and trends at the time, natural topography—" Robbie began, but Sophie stopped him with a gentle touch on his arm.

"He can go on at times," she said with a smile meant to calm.

"It's just…scary. Even down to that slope at the end of the yard. I think that's where I fell because it was dark and I didn't see it," she admitted, recalling the memories that had come to her the night before.

"Diego and his K-9, Poppy, are already at the location you pinned. Hopefully, he can follow your scent from the trail to that home," Sophie said.

Mark leaned forward, hands resting on his muscled thighs, and said, "He needs to hang back from that location, though. If it is the house where WITSEC was holding her—"

"They won't like intruders, but if it's an official location, why was she bound like that? Probably not standard operating procedure for a witness," Jackson said and glanced her way, his gaze drifting to her wrists.

She peered there also and noticed the red bands left by the zip ties. "I was bound. Not in a good way," she recalled. "I was afraid. I knew I had to get away or something bad might happen."

A long, pregnant silence filled the air after her statement because they all seemed to realize what her memories might mean.

"If a marshal was turned—" Mark began, and Jackson finished for him.

"He was going to disappear her. It wasn't an epic fail. It was intentional that she'd go missing. Only she spoiled that plan by escaping."

"This is the man who might be responsible," Robbie said, and popped up a page from the US Marshals website.

Her breath fled again at the sight of his face. The older man she vaguely remembered. "I've seen him."

Mark examined her features as he said, "Was he the one who zip-tied you?"

She closed her eyes and scrounged through what few memories she had. Shaking her head, she said, "I don't know. He doesn't make me too scared, but… I know he's not a friend."

"If this is his assignment, he knows it's gone south. He's trying to find her before anyone else does," Jackson said and then returned his attention to his cousins.

"What do we know about him?"

"US Marshal Jack Rossi. Started as an army grunt before being accepted to West Point. During his service, he eventually became a company commander. After separating from the army, he provided security consulting services to the DOD. Once he left that position, he was elected sheriff and served for nearly a decade until his appointment to the US Marshals service," Sophie said.

"That's quite a résumé," Mark said with a low whistle.

"Is there more you can find out?" Jackson said and grimaced, obviously uneasy with digging into anything more personal.

The siblings shared a look and then nodded. “There are lots of things we can search. Financials. Family connections. Just say the word,” Robbie said, almost too eagerly.

With a heavy sigh, Jackson said, “We need to know everything. Family. Financials. Complaints or problems during his term as sheriff. Any issues as a soldier. But nothing that requires a warrant. If you need one of those, I can arrange it with a local judge.”

It made sense if they wanted to use anything they gathered as evidence, she thought. They wouldn’t want to violate the marshal’s Fourth Amendment’s protections against unreasonable searches and seizures.

And why do I know that? she thought for what had to be the thousandth time.

As fearful as she had been yesterday, frustration was becoming a much more common feeling as time passed.

She wanted—no, she needed—to know what was happening to her and why.

“Thank you for everything you’ve found out,” she said, grateful for what they were doing on her behalf.

“The sooner we get the info, the quicker we can safeguard you,” Mark said, wrapping an arm around her shoulders and giving her a reassuring squeeze.

“We’ll wait to hear more, and thanks again,” Jackson said and ended the meeting.

“Lots of info,” Mark said, taking in everything CPS had been able to assemble from the information he’d sent.

“If I had to bet, I’d say we’ll be hearing from Marshal Rossi sooner rather than later. In the meantime, I’m going to reach out to people I trust and see what I can find about him,” Jackson said and shot to his feet.

Mark also stood and walked with his boss to the door. "I'll let my fingers do the walking," he said and mimicked typing on the laptop. "If there's been an incident while he was sheriff, there may be a news article about it."

Jackson nodded and paused by the door to peer back at their guest as she sat on the couch, head downturned. She was rubbing her thighs nervously again, obviously still worried.

"My gut tells me we need to find out more and soon," Jackson said in tones so low only Mark could hear.

He couldn't disagree. He was starting to feel as if they were sitting on a powder keg with a very short fuse. "Be careful, Jax. If Rossi has been turned, he could be very dangerous."

With a dip of his head, Jackson acknowledged the warning. "I'll keep you posted on anything I find out."

"I'll do the same," Mark said, and with that, Jackson hurried out the door.

Mark ambled back to the couch and sat. "I'm going to find out more about Rossi."

She glanced at him and released a frustrated sigh. "I want to help. It's frustrating to sit here doing nothing. I'm not used to that."

"What are you used to?" he asked, hoping that more of her memories were returning and that it might help them with this investigation.

Her delicate shoulders shifted up and down in a shrug of exasperation. "Dunno, although when you were talking about the warrant, I knew why you needed it."

With his own shrug, he said, "Anyone who watches cop shows knows."

"That it's the Fourth Amendment?" she challenged with the arch of a perfectly manicured brow.

He'd give her that. "Maybe not. So a lawyer?" he asked, inclining his head in a way that invited her to consider it.

She pursed her lips and shook her head. “No, I don’t think so.”

“Cop?” he asked, which might explain how she knew to escape the zip ties.

Closing her eyes, she considered it for long moments. When she opened her eyes and met his gaze, unshed tears glistened there. “I don’t know. Right now, my brain is filled with images of Rossi’s face and that house.”

“It’s a start,” he said and jerked a thumb in the direction of the kitchen table.

“I’m going back to work,” he said. He left her alone to hopefully remember something that might assist them.

As he was about to sit, his phone rang. Diego was calling.

“Buenos dias,” he said. The other cop was not only helping him train Rocky and the other K-9s for their new division, he was also teaching Mark Spanish.

“Buenos dias for sure. Poppy picked up her scent and we’ve tracked it through the underbrush,” Diego confirmed.

“You got Jax’s warning about the possible location?” Mark said, worried for his friend.

“I did, but we’re still a few miles away. Your girl covered a lot of ground through some rough terrain,” Diego said with a surprised breath.

He wanted to say “She’s not my girl,” but held back since he didn’t quite know what to call her.

“Don’t do anything risky,” Mark warned.

“I won’t. I should be able to confirm what her initial location was in another mile or so with my binoculars,” Diego said.

“Great. ¡Cuídate! Adios,” he said, and ended the call.

“It’s ¡Cuídate!,” she said from across the room, correcting his mangled pronunciation of the word.

He narrowed his gaze. “You know Spanish?”

“Supongo que sí,” she replied.

“I guess that means ‘yes,’” he said, slightly puzzled.

"And I guess that means you're just learning Spanish," she said with a light laugh and shake of her head.

"Pretty much. Diego taught me some key phrases for now. Maybe you can teach me some more," he said, and examined her again in light of the revelation.

Her hair was medium brown with caramel highlights, probably from a hairdresser. Creamy white skin with a slight blush, maybe from his perusal, and those eyes. Bright blue and inquisitive.

"We're not a stereotype," she lashed out at his scrutiny. "We're a rainbow of colors and ethnicities."

"Yeah, Diego is trying to teach me that also," he said with a self-deprecating laugh and shake of his head. "His dad is Mexican, but his mom is Spanish. She looks a lot like you, come to think of it."

"Maybe I am, too," she said and seemed to be considering it, but then shrugged. "Who knows?"

Someone does, he thought, and sat to work, wondering what other little tidbits would leak out of that break in her mental dam, a stingy drop at a time.

But a drop at a time can erode even the hardest stone, he reminded himself, and pushed away negative thoughts.

They'd accomplished nothing, and he had a lot to do.

US MARSHAL JACK ROSSI stood in front of the Regina Police Department stationhouse.

It looked like something out of a 1950s movie set in small-town America.

Flowers in a riot of pink, blue, and white lined the steps of what looked like a Craftsman-style building. If not for the large wooden sign mounted about the gabled roof, it might pass as just another of the shops or homes lining Main Street.

Maybe that was the intention, he thought as he walked up the steps onto a narrow front porch and then into a small lobby area.

That was where all traces of small town seemed to disappear, as he examined the neat-as-a-pin lobby, gated security entrance, and the area beyond where several officers worked at what looked like state-of-the-art computers in the bullpen.

He approached the desk, pulling out his badge to hold it up to the older male desk sergeant sitting there.

The man's eyes widened slightly as he perused the round, shiny, silver badge with its star and red, white, and blue shield at the center, and blue letters that said, "United States Marshal."

"I'd like to speak to Chief Whitaker," he said and slipped on the metal chain lanyard with his badge holder so it would be prominently visible to one and all in the station.

The man nodded, pushed a few buttons, and announced his arrival. With a dip of his head, he said, "One of our officers will escort you to the chief."

Barely seconds later, a young policewoman left her desk, came to the gated entrance, and badged the turnstile to unlock it.

"Marshal Rossi. Please follow me," said the officer, whose nameplate identified her as Sergeant Alvarez.

She led him through the bullpen, and he didn't fail to notice all the computers had privacy screens in place to avoid prying eyes.

Interesting, he thought. Not normally what he would expect in such a small department, but then again, Whitaker had connections to Crooked Pass Security.

He'd done his research on the chief and CPS, so he shouldn't have been surprised that they'd be on the ball when it came to technology. But his gut tightened a little since that meant they wouldn't be pushovers just because he was a US marshal. The Whitaker family and their Gonzalez cousins had both the knowledge and connections to blunt any pressure he might exert.

Which might make it difficult to recover his witness if Whitaker and his family had found her.

The sergeant stopped at an interview room. "Make yourself at home," she said.

Interesting again, he thought. Despite her friendly tone, he was definitely being treated like a suspect, which had him wondering if the chief would be recording their interview.

Did that mean they knew why he was there? That they already had the woman in custody?

"Welcome to Regina. I'm Chief Jackson Whitaker," said the man who walked into the interview room and closed the door behind him.

He was tall and powerfully built. Late thirties at the most. Young to be police chief, but Rossi had seen his impeccable record in the military and as a beat cop and detective.

"How can I be of assistance?" Whitaker added and held his hand out in greeting.

He shook the chief's hand tightly and identified himself. "Marshal Jack Rossi. I'm currently assigned to Witness Protection in this area."

"I don't recall getting any notification from WITSEC about any witnesses needing protection in our area," the chief said, his demeanor as calm as a duck on a lake. But everyone knew that beneath that calm, the duck might be paddling furiously.

"This is a very high-profile case," Rossi said.

"Noted. What do you need from us?" Whitaker said, still seemingly helpful.

Rossi set his leather portfolio on the desktop, opened it, and handed Whitaker a file. He hated sharing the information, but with the woman loose and no clues on where she might be, he needed the chief's help. He needed the woman under his control.

The chief perused the file, nonchalantly skimming through the various papers before closing the file. He handed it back, but Rossi held his hand up to stop him.

"Consider yourself notified that Amanda Alonso is in WITSEC in this area. If you get a hint of anything out of the ordinary, advise me ASAP," Rossi said and slid his business card across the table.

The chief seemed a little puzzled then, the first indication that his calm might be a facade.

"Is there anything we should keep an eye out for?" Whitaker asked, but it was almost like he already knew something was up and wanted Rossi to acknowledge it.

Rossi shook his head. "Like I said. Very high-profile and we can't let anything go wrong."

Like it already had, he thought.

Whitaker nodded. "Noted. We'll keep an eye out and let you know if we spot anything out of the ordinary."

He'd make a good poker player, Rossi thought as he stood. "We'd appreciate that."

The chief walked to the door of the interview room, opened it, and gestured for him to exit.

He did and ambled back through the bullpen, Whitaker guarding his back.

As he reached the security gate, he turned and said, "I don't recommend messing with the US Marshals."

Whitaker eyed him, his gray gaze hard and stormy. "That almost sounds like a threat."

"Take it any way you want, Chief. But now would be a good time to tell me if there's anything I should know."

A sharp laugh escaped Whitaker, and he held his hands up in seeming apology. "I'm just a small-town police chief. I'm sure you marshals have got this covered."

With a dismissive huff, Rossi pushed through the security gate and hurried out the door of the police station.

He had no doubt Whitaker knew more than he was saying. Because of that, he'd hang back and see what was up with the police chief. Even if it took all day.

Sauntering to the commonplace sedan parked across from the stationhouse, he hunkered down to wait, certain that Whitaker would lead him to the woman.

Chapter Nine

Mark's cell phone blared Jackson's ringtone.

He answered, but before he could greet his friend and boss, Jackson said, "Are you somewhere private?"

Mark peered to where their guest was sound asleep on the sofa. "No. Give me a second," he said, not wanting to risk her overhearing anyway.

He rushed away and, with a hand command, instructed Rocky to follow. Might as well let the dog get some fresh air.

Rocky sped past him as he opened the sliding door, stepped outside, and closed it.

"What's up?" he asked.

"I sent you some info courtesy of Marshal Rossi. He came to tell me they have a WITSEC witness in our area."

It was easy for Mark to read between the lines. "It's the woman, and I'm guessing Rossi didn't admit she was missing."

"Bingo," Jackson said, and quickly added, "I didn't blink when he showed me her file, but I think he suspects we know more."

"He's trying to hide their failure to protect her or someone on his squad," Mark said.

"Or he's dirty and trying to silence her before she testifies," Jackson tossed out.

Mark hesitated, considering that possibility while Rocky happily loped around the yard.

Finally, he said, “If we go with the latter, we need to safeguard her until we can prove Rossi is dirty.”

“Agreed. Take a look at her file. I’ve sent it to CPS also, so they can dig up more info. I’ll be by later this afternoon to discuss it,” Jackson said.

He was about to hang up when Mark blurted out, “What about the woman? Do I share the information with her?”

A long silence followed. “I’d wait on that. I want to reach out to Ricky Gonzalez, one of the Miami cousins, about her memory loss. He’s a psychologist and may be able to tell us how to handle it.”

“Got it,” he said, then ended the call and walked over to clean where Rocky had relieved himself.

As Rocky and he returned to the kitchen, Mark realized the woman had risen from her nap.

Her gaze met his, and a sad smile slipped across her features. “I wish I had gone out with you. I’m so tired of being cooped up.”

He hesitated, worried it wouldn’t be safe, but then reconsidered, especially since Rocky needed more robust activity than he’d been getting. As for the file Jackson had sent, it could wait since it would be hours before his boss came over for the meeting with CPS.

“No problem. Rocky would love to play some more,” he said, and motioned to the sliding door.

She hurried over, but he stopped her, wanting to check the space just in case.

He walked out with Rocky, perused the area, and, satisfied it was clear, gestured for her to exit.

SHE STEPPED OUT and immediately raised her face to the warm spring sun. Closing her eyes, she savored the precious moment of freedom. A slight breeze drifted around her, bringing the sweet scents of honeysuckle and roses.

A flash of memory had her searching the yard for the honeysuckle.

"Something wrong?" he asked, blue eyes narrowed as he examined her.

With a shrug, she said, "I remembered the smell of the flowers and sucking on one. It was sweet. Someone was with me when I did it, but I can't remember who."

"A friend? Sibling?" he asked, gaze intense.

She did another shrug. "Not sure. Maybe if I taste one, it'll come back," she said and didn't wait for him to hurry across the yard to the vine. She found a fresh flower, plucked it off, and sucked out a bit of the nectar.

The slightly sweet flavor teased her tongue, just as she remembered. She laughed, glad for the memory, no matter how muddled.

He approached, and at his puzzled gaze, she plucked a flower and held it out to him. "Try it."

Mark accepted the flower, brought it to his lips, and tasted the nectar. He smiled and said, "I haven't done that since I was a little boy. Forgot how it tasted."

"I did too, only… I wish it had helped more," she said, sadness sliding in to destroy the happy moment.

Mark cupped her jaw and ran his thumb across her cheek, his touch gentle. "One step at a time."

She wasn't quite as optimistic, but she refused to wallow in pity. Bending, she picked up a small stick and waved it in the air to get Rocky's attention. The large dog immediately understood, and when she tossed the stick, he raced to retrieve it and return it to her.

Taking it from his mouth, she handed it to Mark, worried she shouldn't mess with his working dog.

"Go ahead and play with him."

She nodded at his approval and tossed the stick over and over until her arm began to ache.

Pausing, the dog lay at her feet and looked up at her optimistically, hoping she'd continue. Instead, she bent and rubbed Rocky's large head and shoulders. "Sorry, boy. My pitching arm is a little sore."

"Why don't we go back in. I have some work to do," he said, and she followed him back into the house, but she couldn't go back to that sofa and just sit there mindlessly.

"I was going to start dinner. Is that okay?"

With a dip of his head, he approved, and as she walked to the kitchen, he took a spot at the laptop on the table. She didn't fail to notice that from where he sat, he could see both her and the two entry points into the home.

Always on duty. She got it. When her father…

She stopped short as she was opening the door, remembering a man in blue coming home with a big bouquet.

"You okay?" he asked, catching her hesitation.

"I'm okay," she said, wanting to embrace that happy memory a little longer before sharing it. Wishing that the recollection would expand, so she would see the woman lucky enough to get the flowers. She wanted to spot herself in that vision in the hope it might explain more about who she was.

She opened the door to the fridge, searching for that night's dinner ingredients, but also using it as a shield from his observant eyes as she fought to recover more of that memory.

But the mental scene dissolved as quickly as snowflakes on a wet sidewalk. Her one hope was that more images would come soon and create something that she could build on to recover who she was.

They'd finished the stew for lunch, but there were still many mushrooms, carrots, and potatoes left.

A large package of ground meat screamed at her to make hamburgers, but there weren't any rolls around.

Scrounging through the cabinets, she noticed several boxes of pasta.

Perfect, she thought. The mushrooms, carrots, and meat would make a great base for a Bolognese sauce.

How to cook was something she did remember, and was about to get started when she caught his look from the corner of her eye.

Troubled, she thought. She wondered at it, but let him be, certain that she'd find out soon enough what it was about.

In the meantime, she'd cook and hope that, as they had before, more memories would return. Certain that the man she'd seen holding that immense bundle of flowers had been her father.

MARK PEERED AT her hard, puzzled by what he was reading compared with what he knew of her so far.

Amanda Alonso. The Alonso name might explain how she knew Spanish. The bio in Rossi's packet indicated that her father was Mexican while her mother was Cuban. Her parents were both dead, killed in an automobile accident several years earlier, right after she'd graduated from college. Her father had been a cop, her mother a teacher.

He told himself that their deaths might have made her vulnerable and possibly susceptible to the influence of a slightly older tech entrepreneur who was already making a name for himself in venture fund circles. A handsome man in a nerdy kind of way.

Kind of like you, the little voice in his head teased.

Not that he'd want to be involved with a woman like Amanda Alonso.

Amanda wasn't just a witness. She'd been actively involved in a fraud scheme that had stolen hundreds of millions of dollars from an assortment of investors, including several law enforcement and union retirement funds.

Worse, as the net had been closing around her boss and then boyfriend, Amanda had denied her involvement until the very end. The authorities suspected that she'd used that time to squirrel away millions in untraceable accounts. Despite that, the Feds had made a deal with her to nab her boss in the hopes of recovering where he'd hidden the remaining hundreds of millions stolen from the investors.

As he read through the file, it became clear that large sums of money had been funneled into various political campaigns, possibly to coerce people not to investigate his dealings.

Many more millions had ended up in the accounts of businesses owned by the venture fund head. From there, the money had disappeared.

But apparently, Amanda had helped with all those complicated and secretive transactions. If anyone could untangle the deceitful web of dealings and help recover some of the money, it would be Amanda.

Hence, the offer to go into WITSEC in exchange for her help and testimony.

He leaned back and stared over at her as she cooked.

She seemed more peaceful than she had been before. Untroubled. Was it because she truly couldn't remember or because she was conning him the way she had so many others in her position as the venture fund's chief financial officer?

But then he recalled her injuries and her real fear at being found, as well as her nightmare. There had been anguish there, he told himself, wanting to believe her memory loss was real and not just a ruse.

He shifted forward again, intent on researching the fraud that had occurred. As he did so, the chair creaked, drawing her attention.

Her brows furrowed as she looked his way. "Something wrong?"

He knew Jackson would be pissed with what he was about to do, but he did it anyway.

"Nothing's wrong, Amanda."

The furrow deepened, and she shook her head. "Amanda?"

Not a quiver or twitch to say the name had meant anything. Backing off, he said, "Sorry. You remind me of a distant cousin, and her name's Amanda. Does it sound familiar?"

"Amanda," she repeated and looked upward and to the right, as if searching her memory.

Or lying, the little voice reminded. Looking to the right meant she was creating a story instead of recalling an actual event.

With a little shake of her head, she said, "I've heard that name before. I just can't remember where."

He didn't say, as he had so many times before, that she'd eventually remember because maybe she wouldn't if she was playing the long game.

Instead, he hopped on the internet to read what he could about the venture fund fraud.

AMANDA, SHE THOUGHT as he went back to work.

There was something familiar about the name, but it was also confusing. Her gut said she should remember it, that it was important. And yet the memory hid from her, as if remembering would open a Pandora's box better left closed.

As the knife slipped and nicked her finger, she muttered a curse beneath her breath and dropped the knife.

"Everything okay?" he asked from across the room.

"Fine. Just a little cut," she said, and he was immediately in action, hurrying over to examine the injury.

"It's nothing," she said, but he searched through the cabinets until he located adhesive bandages and alcohol pads.

"Let's clean it first," he said, and immediately cleaned and covered the cut.

"I'm sorry," she said as he wrapped the bandage around it.

He met her gaze, and it was clear he saw it was about more than the small injury.

Cradling her cheek, he stroked his thumb there to soothe her. "What aren't you saying?" he said, as if reading her mind.

"I should remember that name. My gut says I should," she said and tapped her midsection with her fingers.

That gentle touch came on her cheek again. "Is it possible you're blocking that memory? That remembering might be hurtful or upsetting?"

An uneasy feeling erupted between her shoulders with his words.

He knew more than he was saying, and that didn't sit well with her.

She was about to call him out on it when the alarm blared that they had a visitor.

A second later, Jackson walked in, his features set in stern lines that only deepened as he saw them huddled close together.

Mark immediately ripped his hand away from her face, aware of how the scene might look.

Chapter Ten

With an arch of a sandy-colored brow, Jackson said, "Is something wrong?"

Mark stepped back from Amanda and gestured to her bandaged finger. "She cut herself. I was just tending to it."

A dubious look flashed across Jackson's face before he schooled his features.

He reset the alarm and motioned for them to join him in the living room. "CPS is going to call in a few minutes."

With a nod, he walked beside Amanda to the couch, where they sat side by side. Jackson took a wing chair adjacent to them, and as he did so, he said, "We had a visit from US Marshal Rossi this morning. He's the man you think looks familiar."

Amanda nodded. "Yes. You showed me his photo yesterday."

Jackson stared at her, his look a mix of hard and sympathetic. "Rossi left us info that we're going to share with you. It might be troubling," he warned.

An understatement, Mark thought, and laid a gentling touch on her back.

"Troubling? How?" she asked, muscles tense beneath his hand.

Jackson skipped his gaze to him and then back to Amanda. "Rossi advised that a woman in the WITSEC program was in our area. At least that's the reason he gave."

"You didn't believe him," Amanda said, no question in her tone.

"No, I didn't. That woman is you, and there's no way that Rossi doesn't know you're missing," Jackson said, and then quickly tacked on, "He's been watching the stationhouse all day. He tried to follow me, but I ditched him several blocks away."

"What aren't you saying?" Amanda asked, obviously picking up on Jackson's vibes.

"You're not just a witness," Mark said, forcing a sympathetic tone.

"I'm a criminal? I'm not a criminal," she said, a rising note of disbelief in her voice.

Jackson's phone chirped at that moment, warning that CPS was calling.

He snapped on the television and with a few swipes, the faces of Robbie and Sophie Whitaker filled the screen.

Sophie fixed her gaze on Amanda and said, "Jackson sent us a file earlier. Has he shared that info with you yet?"

Amanda shook her head. "He was about to explain."

Sophie's gaze grew almost sympathetic. "This may be difficult to hear, but it's important to go over all the details if we're going to find out what happened to you."

A shudder traveled across Amanda's body, and Mark stroked her back again, trying to comfort her. No matter what the file had said, he was finding it difficult to think of her as a hard-hearted criminal.

"I'm ready," she said and gripped her thighs tightly, as if trying to keep control.

With a nod, Sophie went through the materials he had read earlier, providing the details of the fraud and Amanda's role in it. With each fact revealed, Amanda's body jumped, as if she were being physically pummeled. Finally, when Sophie had finished with Rossi's materials, Amanda collapsed into the sofa cushions as if physically drained.

"THAT'S NOT ME. I couldn't do that. I couldn't," Amanda said and shot up on the cushions. Touching her hand to a spot over her heart, she said, "I know it in here. I could not do that."

"The evidence says otherwise," Jackson said and nailed her with his gaze.

"The evidence is wrong. I did not do that," she insisted, because she knew deep down inside that she was one of the good guys.

The group gathered around all shared a glance before Robbie plowed on. "Let's say you didn't, Amanda."

Amanda. Her name. It was why it sounded familiar, and yet it bothered her to be called that at the same time.

She shot an accusatory glance at Mark. "You don't have a cousin Amanda, do you?"

He shook his head, a hangdog look on his handsome features. "No, I don't."

She had thought she could trust him, but clearly she couldn't.

Something came over her then. Something strong and powerful. She had to take care of herself.

"What other information do you have?" she asked, preparing herself for whatever they had to say and whatever she had to do to get to the truth.

With a nod, Robbie offered additional information to that provided by Rossi.

"The fraud was huge and touched all sectors. Big financial types, as well as an assortment of retirement funds. Nearly one billion dollars was funneled to shell companies, secret accounts, and political PACs."

"Did they recover any of the money?" Mark asked.

"Some, but not nearly enough. They're selling assets to try and make the investors whole, but it will be pennies on the dollar," Robbie explained.

"What about the political PACs? Are they returning the money?" Jackson asked.

Robbie guffawed. "Good luck with that."

Anger stirred in her gut, another sign that she couldn't be guilty of what they had said.

"What about what I allegedly took? Did they go after that?" she asked.

"They did recover funds in some US banks, and your home and other assets have been seized," Sophie explained.

"But not the money I supposedly sent to secret accounts?" she pressed.

"No, not that money. They suspect it's in Cayman Islands accounts," Sophie said.

She shook her head, trying to dislodge any recollections of how to even open a secret account like that, but the only image that came to her was of trying to balance her checkbook and failing.

"I don't know how to do that," she said, honesty dripping from her voice, which seemed to surprise everyone.

"I don't, and I'll say it again. I didn't steal that money. I didn't hide it anywhere," she insisted.

"Again, let's go with what info we have," Robbie said and did a final rundown on what the authorities knew about the monies and activities of the fraudulent venture fund.

"Thanks for that. What did you find out about Rossi?" Jackson asked.

"Family man and loving husband," Sophie said, and displayed assorted images. A wedding photo of Rossi in his army uniform and a beautiful young woman. Family photos of an older version of the couple surrounded by a trio of children. More snapshots with little ones, likely grandchildren, Amanda thought.

"Nothing out of the ordinary in his military career or time at DOD," she said, but then displayed some newspaper articles. "Some complaints about officers in his department using excessive force or racial profiling. Rossi allowed extensive reviews and public discussion on the events, and at the end, the complaints were dismissed."

"Makes it seem like he's a good guy who's not afraid of scrutiny," Mark said.

"That's what we see so far," Sophie said, and what looked like credit reports appeared on the screen.

"Some debts. Nothing out of the ordinary," Sophie advised.

Despite that, Amanda picked up on what she wasn't saying. "You found an issue?"

With a dip of her head, she said, "Being in law enforcement doesn't pay as much as being a politician with a PAC. Rossi's almost at retirement age, but it might not be an easy retirement, especially since his retirement fund invested in—"

"The fake venture fund," she said as the pieces of the puzzle came together.

"Which might make him want revenge—" Mark began, and Jackson finished with, "Or a piece of the money that Amanda has in her secret accounts."

"Or both," Robbie said. "Get the money and then get rid of the witness."

Amanda peered at her wrists, where the red marks from the zip ties were still visible.

Had he been holding her to get the info? she wondered.

MARK DIPPED HIS head so he could see Amanda's face and decipher what she was thinking or feeling.

"Did he hurt you while you were captive? Pressure you for info?" he asked, thinking that he might have tortured her for access to the bank accounts.

A slow back-and-forth of her head communicated her doubt. "I don't know. I don't think so."

Which didn't make sense, he thought, and pressed the issue. "If he didn't pressure her somehow to get the info, why did he take her captive? And what if it wasn't him?"

"He's the main person responsible for getting her to the

courthouse to testify before she serves her prison sentence," Jackson said.

"A prison sentence? You might have mentioned that earlier," Amanda said, a mixture of bite and humor in her voice.

"Two years. A slap on the wrist, all things considered," Jackson said with an annoyed twist of his lips.

"Rossi is in charge, but he must have other agents working with him," Mark said, pushing on with their investigation.

"You're right, Mark. He's not working on this alone," Jackson said and peered at his cousins.

"We're still working on that. Once we have the names of the agents on his team, we will do a deep dive into them as well," Robbie advised.

"Their names might not be an easy thing to find out," Jackson said.

"It won't, but my fiancé is a Colorado Bureau of Investigation agent. He may be able to ask around for that info," Sophie said.

"Or we can ask Rossi outright if we can eliminate him as a suspect," Mark said, hoping that his earlier read of him as a good guy had not been a mistake.

"We can. Thanks for all this. We'll wait for more from you and share anything that we come across," Jackson said, and they ended the call.

Jackson shifted slightly to look his way. "Keep on searching to see what we can find."

Mark nodded as Jackson peered at Amanda. "I know you're having a tough time handling this, Amanda."

"It's not me. I would not do what you've said," she challenged again.

Sucking in a deep breath, Jackson expelled it slowly. With a bob of his head, he said, "I know you believe that. A head injury can do that. All I ask is that you stay open to the possibility it's the truth."

Amanda's body stiffened beside him, not giving him much hope that she would stay open.

Jackson noted it, too. He rose and jerked his head in the direction of the door, signaling that it was time for him to go.

Mark walked him to the door, where Jackson paused and looked back at Amanda.

"Let's hope she remembers something soon. I'm not sure how much longer I can put off Rossi."

"I'll do what I can," Mark said. He disarmed the alarm and slowly opened the door so he could check the area before Jackson walked out.

He had barely cracked it open when the ping-ping-ping of metal on metal registered.

"Get down," he shouted just as the front windows of the home shattered as bullets tore through them. A second later, the screech of car wheels sounded as a car took off.

Mark slammed the metal door and raced toward where Amanda had dropped to the ground between the sofa and the coffee table.

"Are you okay?" he asked even as Jackson rushed out the door, gun drawn.

"I'm fine," she said, and with that, Mark issued a command to Rocky, who had hopped to his feet with the gunfire.

They followed Jackson as he chased after a car screaming away down the block.

Jackson jogged to a stop and holstered his weapon since it was clear he'd never catch the vehicle or have a clean shot.

"Did you get the plate numbers?" Mark asked as he stared after it, Rocky sitting beside him.

"I only caught partial plates, and the make after they raced away. Hopefully, the camera on the house got video of the car and the shooter," Jackson said.

Mark glanced toward the safe house, which was not so safe anymore. "We'll have to move Amanda."

Jackson nodded. "Let me get a BOLO on that car and backup. I'll call CPS and find out if they have a safe house we can use."

Mark hurried away, determined to make sure Amanda really was all right, both physically and emotionally.

When he entered the room, she was huddled on the couch amid the bits and pieces of blown-out glass and wooden shards from the windows, arms wrapped around herself until her gaze connected with his.

Something seemed to travel over her then.

She lifted her chin a defiant inch, stood tall, and dropped her arms to her side. "I am not going to let anyone stop me from doing the right thing."

He didn't doubt that, even though it didn't jibe with the picture of the woman who had emerged from Rossi's report and what CPS had dug up.

This was a very different woman, he thought.

Could a head injury do that? he wondered, but that idea was cut short as Jackson rushed back in.

"CPS sent me the address of a safe house. We should pack up and go."

She didn't hesitate, walking to her bedroom to get her new belongings.

He did the same, hurrying to grab the items Rhea had gathered. He tossed them into a shopping bag before grabbing his backpack and slipping on a jacket.

Jackson waited for them in the open-space area, and as Amanda emerged, she walked over and handed him her bag. Then she went to the stove, shut off the gas, and grabbed the pot of sauce.

At Jackson's questioning glance, she tilted her head up and in a tone that brooked no disagreement said, "I worked hard on this. No one is going to make me leave it behind."

With that, Mark walked over, did a little twirl of his index finger, and said, "Hair, please."

She set the pot down only long enough to twist her hair up into a topknot that Mark tucked into a baseball cap to hide her identity. For good measure, he took sunglasses from his jacket pocket and slipped them on her face. They were oversize and hid most of her delicate features.

At the door, Jackson peered toward the street. "Backup is here."

As he stepped out, Mark noted two squad cars keeping people back. The gunfire had pulled them out of their homes since it wasn't typical in their very peaceful and safe town.

Jackson and he took positions around the pot-carrying Amanda, shielding her from danger and scrutiny. They got her quickly bundled into Mark's Jeep, but he worried that whoever had found this safe house might have placed a tracker on his 4x4.

As he slipped behind the wheel, he said, "We should change out my car at the station in case there's a tracker."

Jackson nodded. "We'll take Rhea's car. I had taken it in for service, and it's at the station."

They hurried to make the switch, and then Jackson drove down Main Street to the highway to reach the location provided by Crooked Pass Security.

It wasn't a long trip, but tension filled him as he kept an eye out for any signs that they were being followed.

At one point, he noticed a small, barebones sedan that had stayed on their tail for several miles, but it turned off the rambling side street onto a private drive. He got a partial plate before it turned and would check to see if the car belonged to the owners of that property, just to be safe.

The home was only about twenty minutes outside town and situated next to one of the larger streams that fed the lake in Regina, which drew so many people during the summer months.

As Jackson pulled into the driveway of what appeared to

be a beautiful vacation home, Mark noted the presence of the cameras on every corner of the house. He also suspected that they'd tripped some kind of driveway alarm as Jackson's phone blared to life.

Chapter Eleven

"I see that you've arrived," Sophie said once Jackson answered.

Their eyes locked as his boss said, "We have."

"No one followed you. There's no activity near the turn for the private road. Nothing going on around the property," she said.

"Cameras?" Mark asked.

"Cameras and other detectors. Get settled, and we'll give you access to all the security features," Sophie advised.

"I've got the alarm codes. We'll phone as soon as we're ready," Jackson said and ended the call.

He exited the car and opened the rear door to escort Amanda to the waterside home.

Mark hung back, grabbing the bags with their clothes and unharnessing Rocky before he did a slow walk to the building, scoping out the area to familiarize himself with the basic setup.

He entered, placed the bags on the floor, and then returned to pick up the pot with the sauce that had meant so much to Amanda.

In a way, he got it. That simple task represented a sense of normalcy that was lacking in her current life.

And maybe in her future life, he thought as he considered what two years in prison would be like. Granted, it would be a minimum-security prison for white-collar types, but the idea of being confined like that caused a spot between his shoulders to itch.

He was just too used to freedom and exploring the glorious mountains, lakes, and streams in the area around Regina.

Once he had brought the pot in and placed it on the stove, Jackson secured the door and set the alarm.

Mark paid careful attention, memorizing the code. Before Jackson left, he'd take Rocky around the property to make sure he knew the terrain for himself, in case of any emergency.

While he and Jackson had been tending to the alarm, Amanda had gone over to the stove to warm the sauce. Dinnertime was only an hour or so away if they wanted to eat before the sun went down. He definitely wanted to get outside and scope out the property before it got dark.

"I should take Rocky around while it's light," he said to Jackson.

"I agree. Let's call CPS and see if they're ready for a meeting," he said and phoned Sophie again.

Mark could overhear that they were ready, and as they had at the other safe house, Jackson flipped on the television to video call with CPS.

Sophie's and Robbie's faces filled the screen. "We hope you made it without any issues," Robbie said.

"Just a sedan that pulled off several miles away. I'm going to run their plates later to make sure there's nothing to worry about," Mark advised.

"We're not seeing anything going on, and we'll have our staff monitoring the various feeds. We'll send you links to an app you can use, plus there's a laptop in the living room to help with monitoring the area," Sophie advised.

"There's a driveway alarm at the entrance and security cameras that will capture any activity around the perimeter of the home. There are also some trail cams in and around the house and the stream area. You may get wildlife activity on those, which might cause a false alarm," Robbie warned.

"Got it. We appreciate the use of the property," Jackson said, and shared a look with him before he said, “Do you have anything else on Rossi or his team?”

“We did a deeper dive on Rossi’s financials. There was a large deposit just about a month ago that seems unusual,” Sophie advised, and a second later, what looked like a bank statement appeared on the screen.

Mark sucked in a breath at the sight of the six-figure deposit. “That’s a nice chunk of cash.”

“It is. We’re researching if there’s a valid excuse for it,” Robbie said.

“We’re still working on getting the names of Rossi’s team. As soon as we have anything, we’ll let you know and investigate them, too,” Sophie said.

“Great. We’ll do our own research as well,” Jackson said.

“Roger that,” Robbie said, and a second later, the screen went dark.

Mark jumped to his feet and did a hand command that had Rocky sidle close.

“Rocky and I are going to scope out the property,” he said, and at Jackson’s nod, he rushed out the door with his K-9.

AFTER STARTING THE sauce again, she had joined the men in the living room and sat there silently, listening to all the protective measures in place and the team’s plan to keep her safe.

As the door closed behind Mark and Rocky, Jackson swiveled in his chair and examined her with a withering look.

“We’re doing what we can, but it would be great if you could do something to help yourself, Amanda,” he said, his tone on the verge of accusatory.

“Do you think I’m willingly not remembering? Do you think it’s easy for me not to know?” she challenged because her insides were in turmoil thanks to the revelations that had happened that day.

Before he could answer, she pressed on, splaying her hand

across her heart. "It's killing me in here to think I might have hurt people. Stolen from them. That's not me. I know deep down inside that it's not me," she urged, wishing that he would believe her because she believed it with all her heart.

Her impassioned defense seemed to have hit home.

Jackson relaxed slightly and inclined his head to acknowledge her plea. "I'll take you at your word…for now. In the meantime, I'm going to check out the app and laptop to see what Mark is doing."

MARK STARTED BY taking a slow walk all around the edge of the home, letting Rocky sniff and explore to familiarize himself with his surroundings.

As he did so, he caught sight of Jackson and Amanda in the living room, obviously engaged in what appeared to be a tense discussion, but he couldn't hear what was being said.

Because he could see them, he turned to examine the area to see if someone could get off a shot through the windows.

That big window faced the stream, which had a few hiding places on their side of the water. The opposite bank was covered in moss, with an area where someone might stand to fish. That open spot was flanked by underbrush and small saplings. Farther back, larger trees and a deeper tangle of vines and small bushes could provide a hiding place, but he noticed something attached to one tree: a trail cam.

CPS had eyes on that area, which provided some measure of relief about a sniper shooting from there.

Satisfied, he continued his surveillance, leading Rocky to the small lawn and raised beds behind the home. Pushing on, he hiked through the area, noticing another trail cam or two before trudging to the home's driveway.

He walked to the end of the drive and the winding road that led up the mountain to several other homes and down to the highway and Regina in the other direction.

The only sounds as he stood there were the slight rustle of leaves as a slight breeze kicked up and the barely there, sibilant sound of the water in the nearby stream.

One set of worries about the security of the location gave way to another: What was happening with Jackson and Amanda?

Amanda had made it clear that she didn't believe she had committed the crimes of which she was accused.

Jackson obviously thought she had.

What about you? the little voice in his head challenged. *Do you believe her?*

His gut told him there was more to her story than what it seemed on its face.

And he had to admit there had been a visceral connection between them from the start. An attraction that he didn't want to explore, but was difficult to ignore. After all, she was a beautiful woman in distress, and that called to him.

His sister had always teased him that he had a soft spot for wounded animals and people who needed saving, and Amanda, in her current state, definitely fit that bill.

Because of that, he took a moment to gird himself against that attraction as he stood at the front door. With a bracing breath, he entered to find Amanda at the stove, lifting a lid off a pot of what looked like boiling water.

"Good timing. It's ready for the pasta," she said with a smile that warmed him despite his best efforts.

"Let me just clean up and feed Rocky," he said as he bent slightly to free the cane corso from his leash.

Jackson walked over as he was pulling some bowls from a cabinet for Rocky's food and water.

His boss and friend jerked a thumb in the direction of the living room. "When you're done, come over. I recorded the feeds from your walk so you can see what the cameras cover," he said.

"Got it," he said, then quickly prepped a station for Rocky

and joined Jackson, who immediately demonstrated what was visible on the app and laptop.

Mark nodded and said, "Looks great. I'll do an in-depth view after dinner. Are you staying?"

Jackson shook his head and then glanced at Amanda and the very domestic image she presented. "No, Rhea's waiting for me as well as quite a few reports on some other cases. But, I think…"

He hesitated as his gaze nailed Mark. "You need to be careful, my friend. She can be convincing."

Mark looked at her again and firmed his lips. "She can, but my gut tells me it isn't an act, Jax."

"I trust your gut. It's why you're my right-hand man, but there's always—"

"A first time to be wrong. I get it. Your concerns are duly noted," Mark said because he valued Jackson's advice.

Jackson clapped him on the back. "Good. I'll talk to you in the morning unless we get something else from CPS tonight."

"Got it. I'll keep on working on it as well," he said and walked Jackson to the front door. Once he'd left, Mark reset the alarm and strolled over to the stove, where Amanda was stirring the pot with the pasta.

He stood beside her, fingers jammed into his jeans pockets to keep from reaching for her.

"How's it going?" he asked and glanced at her.

A mistake. The steam and warmth from the stove had brought a rosy flush to her cheeks. A small smile of satisfaction graced her full lips, tempting him almost as much as the enticing smell from the nearby pot of sauce.

Luckily, the sauce won out as his stomach growled noisily.

"It's going well. I'll take the pasta out in a few minutes and let it finish in the sauce," she said, clearly comfortable with what she was doing.

"It seems as if you cook a lot," he said, hoping to elicit a fresh set of memories.

She had been stirring the pasta, but stopped, considering his comment.

With a nod, she said, "I think I do cook a lot, but I remember eating a lot of fast food also. Like, as if I didn't have time for a real meal."

"You must have worked long hours with Dave," he said, referring to David Peterson, who had run the fake venture fund.

She stopped stirring again, confusion on her face this time. Brows furrowed together, she said, "Dave? I don't think so."

"Sorry. I shouldn't make assumptions," he said, aware he was walking a tightrope. He wanted her to remember, but he also didn't want to implant names and memories that weren't her own.

"I'll go set the table," he said and walked away.

SHE REPEATED DAVE'S name over and over in her brain, but it didn't connect.

Neither did the name Amanda. She'd been repeating that to herself, trying to own it since it was supposedly her name, but it hadn't happened.

She didn't feel like an Amanda, although the more she repeated it, the more familiar it sounded.

As for Dave…

She stopped stirring as something clicked, but a second later the timer dinged and the thought burst like a soap bubble in the wind.

Time to sauce the pasta, she thought, and reserved a little of the pasta water before draining away the rest in a colander.

She obviously cooked a lot. The pasta water wasn't a novice trick, and yet she couldn't explain why she knew you kept it in case you needed to thin the sauce.

But she *did* know that, she thought as she dumped the pasta into the sauce and mixed the two for the last few minutes of cooking.

When the pasta was ready, she spooned out healthy servings and brought the bowls over to the table, where Mark had set out glasses of soda for them as well as some grated cheese.

As she laid the bowls down, he said, "The fridge and freezer are stocked pretty well. They must use this as a weekend place."

She nodded. "Same with the cabinets. I don't think we have to worry about food for our stay." A stay that she hoped wouldn't be too long, not that she'd mind spending time with the handsome cop in other circumstances.

He must have read her mind since he said, "Hopefully, we can get you somewhere safe to testify soon."

Testify and go to prison, she thought, and again it struck her as wrong. Not because she didn't deserve punishment if she'd done the fraud, but more because she remained convinced that she wasn't the kind of person to commit such a crime.

Those clashing thoughts dimmed her appetite, but only for a second, since this was one of her favorite meals. Again, it frustrated her that she could remember that and not much else, but she'd embrace that thought. With any luck, it would bring more.

They ate in silence, hunger the prime motivator, but as they neared the bottom of their bowls, Mark finally said, "You're a great cook. This is delicious."

She smiled at the compliment. "Thanks. It's the mushrooms. I actually make a sauce with just eggplants and mushrooms. I used to be a vegetarian," she said, a slight note of surprise in her voice.

Chapter Twelve

"A vegetarian, huh? I could never give up my steaks," he said, treating it as a throwaway comment even though he'd stored it away in the hope it would lead to some kind of future revelation.

With a bark of a laugh, she said, "Me, either. I think it was a short-lived phase."

"My sister went through a similar one. It only took a Memorial Day weekend and my dad's famous ribs to break her out of it," he said with a broad smile as he remembered how Sarah had dug into the meat with gusto.

She grinned and said, "My sister…"

Her face was filled with surprise at the words she'd uttered. A second later, she shook her head, as if trying to shake free the rest of that memory.

When she didn't continue, he tried to urge her on.

"You have a sister?"

She scrunched her eyes shut, did a slow and deliberate inhale, and held it. With another shake of her head, she met his gaze, and tears shimmered there.

"I think I do, but I can't remember much more. I can't remember her face. How's that possible?" she asked, pain coloring her voice.

He laid a hand on hers as it rested on the table. "It's a start. A good start."

She nodded, and a half smile crept across her lips, but it didn't reach eyes glimmering with tears.

With a wobbly shake of her head, she returned her attention to the last strands of spaghetti in her bowl, and he did the same, finishing what had been a delicious meal.

She really was a good cook, and so far, food had been something that had helped her recover some of her past. Not a surprise since food and the smells associated with it often created powerful associations for people.

Together, they cleaned off the table and placed the dishes and pots in the dishwasher.

While they had eaten and cleaned, night had fallen outside. Since they were in the woods with no artificial lights, the area around the home was quite dark.

He worried the lights from inside would make them too visible, so he drew heavy curtains across the living room windows as a safeguard. As he did so, he realized that the glass appeared thicker than normal.

Bulletproof? he wondered, contemplating why the home had such high-level security features. But then he remembered that the Whitaker parents had been kidnapped months earlier, and as former top NSA operatives, they might be prime targets.

If this were a place the Whitaker family used regularly for themselves, it would explain the security features.

Jackson had left the laptop running, and night vision had kicked in on the various camera feeds. He had yet to review how they had picked him up earlier, and he intended to do so later. But first, he wanted to do another walk across the area to see how someone might use nightfall to pierce the security. It would also be a good test of how alert the new CPS associates were monitoring the cameras.

Facing Amanda, he said, "I'm going to walk Rocky. You may see me on the monitors and hopefully, CPS will as well and call."

He motioned to a phone right next to the laptop. "You can pick up if they do, and I'll let Jackson know what I'm doing so he doesn't worry," he said and shot off a quick text to his friend.

Hurrying to the bedroom, he changed into a darker-colored shirt and jacket. The temperature had likely dipped, and he'd noticed some raspberry vines with sharp thorns that would scratch if he accidentally came in contact.

In the living room, he clicked his tongue and motioned to Rocky, who instantly shot to his feet and hurried over.

He clipped on Rocky's leash and headed to the door, and Amanda met him there and laid a hand on his chest to stop him.

"Please be careful out there," she said, a furrow of worry across her brow.

He ran his finger across it and offered her a big smile. "Don't worry. I've got my weapons with me," he said, then tapped a hand to his holstered pistol and rubbed Rocky's head.

A smile and sigh of relief escaped her. "I'll be waiting for you."

Her words brought an unexpected feeling of home as he headed out the door, vigilant for the cameras that might track him and anything abnormal.

He stayed close to the home, hopefully below the camera's view.

Reaching the one corner, he bent low and urged Rocky into a crouched position as well. Tucked close to the ground, they stayed beneath the edges of some taller underbrush a few feet from the driveway. Moving carefully, he muttered a curse as he caught sight of a trail cam that had likely picked up their movement.

Pressing forward, he pushed toward the road since an attack would most likely come from that area.

The driveway was clear, as was the nearby road. Creeping low, he moved along the ground, hidden by the underbrush.

Satisfied, he started back toward the driveway when he noticed the beam of headlights illuminating the asphalt. It was followed by the crunch of tires from the gravel shoulder.

A second later, the sound and light stopped short.

So wrong, he thought. It had been too close to their property and too far from the drive for the next home down the road.

He hurried to investigate, Rocky tucked close.

They passed the driveway, staying hidden, until he saw the dark outline of a car sitting at the edge of the road.

The headlights were off, and with only a sliver of moon overhead, it was hard to see if anyone was at the wheel. But then the driver's side door opened, and the inside lights snapped on.

A thirtysomething man wearing a ball cap, jacket collar turned up, slipped from the seat quickly, giving Mark only a short glimpse of his face. Not enough that he could pick him out in a lineup, he thought.

The man looked around, as if searching for something, but then went to the back wheel well area.

He bent, disappearing from Mark's view.

He muttered a curse, but didn't dare move forward for a better look, certain that the man might hear the rustle of the underbrush.

Barely a minute later, the man popped up, hurried back to the driver's seat, and started the car.

The headlights snapped on, and he pulled off the softer shoulder onto the hard roadway.

Slowly, the car moved forward, and Mark followed, staying low with Rocky at his side.

At the entrance to their driveway, the car stopped.

Inspecting? Mark wondered, but as he neared, he noticed that the tire on the back driver's side looked a little flat.

Was he looking for a place to ask for help? Mark thought. Cell service could be spotty in areas on the mountain, but not at this low elevation.

The man pulled partly into the drive and Mark unleashed Rocky, readying him in case he needed to issue the attack command. But then the man executed a K-turn on the narrow road and drove back in the direction of town.

Just in case, Mark snapped off a picture of the car and its license plate.

Returning to his reconnaissance of the property, he rushed back, staying low and hopefully out of sight of some of the cameras.

At the house, he headed to the stream area.

Once there, he peered across the running water, judging its depth and the risk of crossing from the other side.

Deep and uneven. A spring rain had water rushing toward the lake and would make a crossing difficult, but not impossible. He stored that bit of information away for safety's sake.

Satisfied with the night's outing, he rose and unleashed Rocky, letting him run loose for the last few yards to the house.

The cane corso was an active dog, and he had to keep his partner in shape both physically and mentally, so he let him wander in and around the front of the house before calling him to return to his side.

When he entered, Amanda was waiting for him by the door, phone in hand.

"They called. Jackson, too. They picked you up a few times," she said, and handed him the phone.

He dialed the number for the most recent call, and a CPS associate immediately answered.

"Good evening, Sergeant Dillon. Robbie and Sophie wanted me to let you know that we recorded your outing tonight," a young woman said.

"Good evening and thanks. Did you pick up anyone besides me in the feeds?" he asked, wondering about the car he'd spotted.

"We did. Black sedan. Late model. We've taken a screenshot of the car and its license plate for you. It's available on the laptop drive, but we can run the plate for you if you want," she said, her tone professional and smart.

"That would be great. Thank you," he said.

When he hung up, he met Amanda's gaze. "Looks like everything is under control."

She nodded and released a long exhale. "That's good to hear."

"I've still got some work to do. I was going to make some tea."

Holding up a hand to stop his move to the kitchen area, she said, "I'll make it so you can work."

"Great, thanks," he said and headed to the living room and the laptop sitting there.

THE MUSCLES OF her body had tightened like an overly wound spring coil when he had left earlier.

Now that he was back, worry disappeared, and that tight coil spiraled open, relaxing every inch of her body.

She went to the kitchen and pulled out a teapot and bags that she had spotted earlier when searching for the pasta.

A teakettle already sat on a back burner. She filled it and set the water to boil in anticipation of steeping the tea.

As she stood there, her reflection in the shiny black of a nearby microwave caught her attention.

She shifted there and stared hard at herself.

Does my sister look like me? she wondered.

In the long minutes while he had been checking the grounds, she'd searched her brain for any memories of her family. A sister, for one. Parents for another.

But no new images had come, much like now.

It was just her face, staring back at her. Nothing that clued her to what her sister might look like.

She asked herself, as she had multiple times that night, *How is that possible?*

But try as she might, no explanation came.

Tears threatened again, but she drove them back. She was done crying about her situation. She had to find a way to help herself.

Pushing away from the microwave, she prepped the teapot, placing a few tea bags in it since she liked her tea almost as strong as coffee.

As the low whistle of the teakettle warned that the water was ready, she grabbed a pot holder and the teakettle. After pouring the boiling water into the teapot, she put the lid back on and waited a few minutes for the tea to steep.

"How do you like your tea?" she called out.

"Cream, light, and sweet."

She hadn't seen any cream in the fridge, but there had been a powdered creamer in a cabinet.

She used that for both their mugs, dumped in a few teaspoons of sugar, and stirred.

Since there was still some tea left in the pot, she wrapped a kitchen towel around it to use as a cozy and then walked over to where he sat in the living room, perusing the video from earlier.

"How's it going?" she asked as she set the cup beside him on the narrow desktop.

"I have a good idea of what's protected," he said and glanced up at her. "Want to see?"

"I do," she said. She wanted to be an active participant in protecting herself.

Mark grabbed a remote and, with a few clicks, streamed the laptop screen to the television.

She sat quietly, scrutinizing the recordings, and something clicked inside her.

Pointing to the videos from the house cameras, she said, "The field of view is good. They must be using a wide-angle lens to get that much distance and width, but they won't get directly underneath the camera."

Mark seemed surprised by her comment, but held back and tapped a few keys to flip to another set of cameras.

Grainy and not all that clear. "These must be from the trail cams. I assume they're motion-activated like most trail cams."

As if to prove her point, one of the cameras snapped to life, sending a feed of a small fawn and her mother sipping water from the far side of the stream.

"Beautiful. That fawn can't be all that old," she said, recalling that most fawns were born in late April to early June in the area.

"Probably a newborn," Mark confirmed, then turned in the desk chair and scrutinized her.

"You know a lot about cameras and deer. Are you a hunter?"

She vehemently shook her head and waved her hands. "No way. I could never shoot an animal…" she began, but then her voice trailed off as a memory slammed into her.

"I've shot a dog. It was going to attack me. So I shot it. With a handgun," she said, her voice sounding far away even to her own ears, as if she wasn't really the person who had done the shooting.

Chapter Thirteen

Nothing in her record had given him a clue that she had a handgun and knew how to use it.

"Keep on going. Was the dog rabid?" he asked, guiding her down the road that had led to that memory.

She shook her head and clasped her fingers tightly in her lap. "No. It wasn't. It was gray and white. Muscular. A pit bull, I think."

"Where were you? Why did you have a gun?" he asked, thinking that the average person wouldn't be carrying a weapon in light of Colorado's strict gun laws.

Closing her eyes, she scrunched her brows together, struggling to remember, but then they popped open, and she shook her head.

"I don't know. I wish I did, but I can't recall anything else," she said, but there were no tears this time. Just a steely tone that said she was fighting hard to change that status.

With a dip of his head, he offered support and returned to the videos of his two outings on the grounds. Nothing popped for either of them, and then he finished with the image of the car that had made the K-turn in the driveway.

The image wasn't as grainy as that from the trail cams, but also not as sharp as that from the cameras on the house. Despite that, a plate was visible, and he made out the badging on the back of the car.

"Ford Fusion," she said, also recognizing the brand, and then added, "A hybrid version. Rewind the video a bit."

He did as she asked, rewinding the video to the start of the turn where, sure enough, the blue, green, and silver badge was visible.

"Good catch. That should limit how many vehicles we have to search, just in case the plate's stolen," he said.

"The plate is from a fleet. See the FLT to the left?" she said, and motioned to the image of the license plate.

Mark frowned. "That could make the driver harder to track down," he said, then reached over and brought out the laptop he had taken from the police's safe house.

"Or it could mean he was a lost tourist and we don't have to worry," she proposed.

"True. We'll confirm the fleet once I access DMV," he explained as he opened the second laptop and logged on.

AMANDA WATCHED INTENTLY as he did it, and his actions and the screens seemed very familiar.

Had she watched one of the marshals use these same services, or had she used them herself? she wondered.

Mark entered the license plate, and it instantly came back as belonging to a rental company working out of Denver International Airport.

"It's one of the small rental companies," he said.

"Either a tourist trying to save money or someone avoiding exposure since a small company doesn't have all the tech bells and whistles of a national chain. No scanned license with a picture," she said as she reviewed the info on the screen.

Mark slowly faced her, examining her features. "Rent a lot of cars lately?" he asked, clearly wondering how she'd arrived at that conclusion.

She sat up slightly, wondering yet again how she knew that.

"Maybe Amanda rents a lot of cars," she said, still thinking of Amanda as some other person since she didn't want to be a criminal like Amanda.

"Maybe," he said, but his tone and body posture said he wasn't quite buying it.

"I'll talk to Jackson about going in the morning," he said, then closed the laptop and reached for his cell phone.

She laid a hand on his arm to stop him. As he met her gaze, puzzled, she said, "*We'll* go in the morning. I'm tired of just sitting here, doing nothing to figure out who I am and why someone wants me gone."

He shook his head vehemently and slashed his hands in the air. "No. No way will I put you at risk like that."

"Can you afford to send another officer out here to babysit me? Will they do as good a job as you?" she challenged.

SHE MADE A lot of sense. But her appeal to his pride about being the best man for the job smelled of being manipulative.

Maybe that skill was one she'd used to convince people to give her the money that she and her boss had stolen.

Still, she was right about losing another officer to watch her if he went to Denver. The department would be short-staffed if that happened.

"I'll agree to it, but not because you played me," he said, making it clear he wasn't falling for her ploy.

Her brows furrowed, and she shook her head. "Played you?"

He held his hands up to his chest and mimicked a sweet, adoring look. In a mock voice, he said, "Oh, Mark. You're the perfect man for this job."

Her body did a little jump, and her features darkened with hurt and anger. "Is that what you think? That I tried to deceive you?"

"Given what we know about you, what would you think?" Mark challenged.

The sheen of tears filled her eyes, but to his surprise, they seemed like real tears of hurt and not a sympathy ploy.

"You know nothing about me. I don't either, except for one thing. I am not that Amanda. I am not that person who hurt so many people," she said, voice thick with emotion.

Her upset stirred something in him. Something alive and dangerous given the situation.

But he couldn't resist reaching up, cradling her cheek, and offering comfort. "It would be a lot easier for us if you could remember more, Amanda."

She slapped his hand away and snapped, "Don't call me that. I'm not that woman."

Her outrage was as real as the pain he'd seen earlier.

"Okay. I won't call you that. What should I call you? Hey, you?" he said, taking hold of her hand and giving a playful shake to lighten the moment.

Her full lips tilted up in an awkward half smile, and a rough laugh escaped her. "Hey, you will work."

With another teasing shake of her hand, he said, "It's late. Why don't you get some rest while I convince Jackson we both aren't completely bonkers."

She nodded, and her smile widened slightly. "That sounds like a plan and…thank you. Sincerely," she said, and laid a hand over her heart. "No matter what we find out, I appreciate all that you're doing."

Damn, she touched something else deep inside him again. But he tempered that reaction, aware that there was still too much he didn't know about her.

"Get some rest," he said, voice gruff with the unwanted emotion she had roused.

"Good night," she said and hurried away.

He waited until she was ensconced in her room, door closed, before he let out a breath and leaned back into the desk chair, considering all that had just happened.

She was so adamant about not being Amanda, and his gut told him that wasn't an act. It truly bothered her.

But a head injury could do something like that. It could change a person's personality. Or even give them traits and information they hadn't possessed before.

Like the knowledge she seemed to have about things like warrants, license plates, or car rental companies.

He'd watched a show recently that talked about acquired savant syndrome, which had highlighted several cases where people had developed new talents after suffering a brain injury or disease.

Is that what is happening with her? He decided to raise the issue with Jackson.

Since it was late and his friend had a new baby at home, he texted him first to see if he was available for a call.

When he got a reply that it was all good, he dialed.

Jackson immediately answered. "Everything okay?"

"Yes, and no," Mark answered honestly and reported on what they'd found out about the mystery car that had visited that night.

"Someone lost on the road, maybe, but it makes sense to check it out. I can send—"

"Me. And Amanda, although she doesn't want me to call her that," he said, and explained about the tortured conversation they'd had.

"It's not easy to admit who or what you are," Jackson said, tone hard and yet sympathetic. But then he quickly added, "But she's not going with you."

"She won't stay here. Trust me. And we can't lose another officer for this assignment. We'd be short-staffed, especially since we're already seeing the first rush of tourist visitors," he said, trying to convince his boss.

A long hesitation was followed by the sounds of his expelled breath. "Go ahead. I just hope this is not a big mistake."

"I'll keep her safe. But in the meantime, do you think you can ask your cousin Ricky for some help again?" he said, priming his friend for his next request.

"Sure, why?" Jackson asked, and in the background, a baby's cry pierced the quiet of the night.

"The woman we have in custody knows things that maybe Amanda wouldn't know. I recently heard about this thing called acquired savant syndrome. It makes people have new skills and talents due to head injuries. Maybe Ricky could give us some more info on that," Mark said as the baby's cries grew ever louder.

"I'll reach out to him, but in the meantime, I've got to go. Axel's hungry," he said.

"Go take care of your little one. Axel's the best," he said. He was almost like an uncle to the little one-year-old boy and often watched him so Jackson and Rhea could have some free time.

"Easy for you to say. You're not the one waking up in the middle of the night," Jackson teased and ended the call.

It was easy for him to say and yet…

He hadn't been involved with anyone seriously for months since he'd been so busy with his new position and working with Diego to train Rocky and start building the department's new K-9 division.

But even with that, he wondered more than once if it wasn't time to start thinking about finding the right woman and building a family with her.

Amanda was not that woman, no matter how she stirred him.

Rocky meandered over then and sat before him, his dark brown eyes almost understanding. But it was also a reminder that he had to take care of his partner before he could shut his eyes for some rest.

He rubbed Rocky's head and said, "You're a good boy. Let's get you some fresh air."

Rising, he signaled Rocky to follow him to the back door, and he opened it to step out with his partner.

Rocky immediately went to the edge of the lawn, almost disappearing into the night thanks to the black of his fur. The dog quickly relieved himself and then returned to Mark's side.

Mark playfully tussled with the large dog, who loved a good massage and a roughhouse. He was grateful Rocky was on his side because he wouldn't want to get into a real fight with a dog that big and powerful.

After grabbing a bright orange hard ball by the back door, a sure sign that Jackson's cousins had a dog and likely used this as a weekend getaway, he tossed it, and Rocky eagerly ran after it. After snaring it in his large jaws, he raced back to return it to Mark and continue their game.

Chuckling, he repeated the toss and retrieve for some time, because Rocky needed the exercise, and truth be told, he needed this mindless activity to clear his brain of so many conflicting emotions.

After a final throw and return of the ball, Mark rubbed Rocky's body vigorously and then signaled him that it was time to go back in.

Ever obedient, the dog followed him to the door, and once they were back in and the alarm reset, he went to his bedroom to change into comfortable sweats before returning to the living room area.

He was too awake to sleep, and he wanted to be able to keep an eye on what was happening on the grounds. For that reason, he took a quick look at the various camera feeds and, satisfied that all was calm, he sprawled on the sofa.

Flipping on the television, he searched for a familiar favorite that might lull him to sleep, or at least a light rest, while he guarded the house.

But just as he found a show, the door to Amanda's room

slowly opened, and she stepped into the room, arms wrapped around herself.

"Hey, you," he said, wanting to keep things light and mindful of her earlier request.

"Hey, you, right back. I couldn't sleep. I was hoping I could hang for a little bit," she said with a hesitant smile.

Chapter Fourteen

Amanda sucked in a breath and held it, expectant. It was risky for them to spend time together because something was growing between them.

He sensed it as well, she knew.

Despite that, he pursed his lips and did a slow dip of his head. "Sure. I was just going to watch some television."

Something she'd grown tired of over the last day because she wasn't used to inactivity.

It struck her again how odd it was that she remembered that and not more important things.

She slowly walked over, and he was about to rise from his spot on the sofa, but she raised a hand to stop him. "No, that's okay. I'll take the chair," she said, guilty that he'd lose his comfortable place, especially since she suspected that he'd planned on spending the night there to keep watch and protect her.

With a smile, he settled back into the cushions, and she sat in the chair, leaned against one arm, and tossed her legs over the other. That brought her head close to his when he lay against the side of the couch.

He smelled fresh and woodsy, like the pine trees in the forest she had traipsed through the day before. But beneath that scent was something masculine and compelling. Comforting as well.

She didn't doubt he'd risk himself and Rocky to protect her.

She did a slow inhale, taking it in because it made her feel good. She didn't think she'd felt good like that in a long time.

The show he'd turned on was a familiar one, and she suspected he'd chosen it because it wouldn't matter if he dozed while he "watched."

Her mom had regularly claimed that she watched television with her eyes closed, she remembered, and that memory brought more comfort, but also sadness. She screwed her eyes shut to resurrect an image of her mother, and as it came, she held on to that recollection.

But as that image faded, another swept in. She was holding hands with another young girl. A sister, she knew, and yet her face remained in shadow. A mystery, as the memory was wiped away like a wave washing over a message written in the sand.

She groaned in frustration, prompting him to say, "You okay?"

As she opened her eyes and faced him, she realized their heads were almost touching as they rested on the furniture.

His green-eyed gaze was sharp. Assessing.

"I remembered my mom. She was so beautiful. And I remembered my sister again only… I can't see her face. It's frustrating."

"I wish I could help you, but your existence has been scrubbed so clean that we know almost nothing about you that's not connected to the case. If that info's available, Rossi didn't give it to us, and CPS couldn't find it. At least not yet," Mark said, sympathetic to her plight.

She nodded. "It's why I need to do more to find out what's happening and why. I don't want to be a *tabula rasa*, a clean slate with no past and no future," she said, needing him to understand why it was so important.

He shifted and stroked a hand along her cheek. His touch, like his scent, comforted. Brought hope for more. Maybe even with someone like him. Hope she wasn't sure it was right to have if she was Amanda. A woman who had selfishly hurt so many.

"It may take time, but we will find out the truth," he said, and the strength of his conviction brought even greater relief to her troubled soul. But it also roused that unwanted emotion again.

She found herself shifting in her seat, leaning toward him until their lips were barely an inch away. His warm breath, minty clean, bathed her lips, inviting her to close the space between them.

His lips were so warm. Hard and mobile as he accepted her invitation. Tasted her until with a groan, he jerked away, eyes wide.

Sitting, he held his hands up in a stop gesture. "This can't happen. We both know why."

"Why?" she said, defying him even though he was right.

She was tired of doing the right thing. An odd thing to think, considering that everything she supposedly knew about herself said she hadn't done the right thing in quite some time.

"I need to stay objective. I can't let emotions interfere with this investigation," he said and darted away, creating what she supposed was needed distance between them.

"Too late, Mark. You might want to deny it, but on some level, you believe me when I say I didn't do all those awful things," she said, urging him to admit what he was feeling.

He rose and paced back and forth for a few seconds before he faced her and raked his fingers through his hair in obvious frustration.

"I believe that *you* believe, but it's only because you can't remember," he said, hands held out in pleading.

She popped up in her chair. "Liar. Your gut says I'm innocent. Don't deny it," she said, daring him to admit the truth in his heart.

Like a balloon deflating, the tension fled his body, and he stood before her, seemingly defeated.

It bothered her more than she would admit. "I'm sorry. You're right. This," she said, gesturing between them, "is wrong right now."

"It is, Amanda," he said, creating even more distance between them with the use of her name. A hated name she refused to take.

I am not that Amanda, she reminded herself and rose. "I'm going back to my room so you can do your thing," she said and gestured toward the sofa, where he had been relaxing before she had intruded.

Head held high, she walked to her bedroom and closed the door behind her.

Her throat choked with emotion, her earlier hopefulness gone thanks to the argument with him. Tears sheened her eyes, blurring her view of the room and making it look like a watercolor painting.

She dashed the tears away, and as she did so, she realized that while she couldn't escape the emotions creating her turmoil, she could escape him.

Behind the curtains at the far wall of the room was a sliding door to the backyard.

She'd trip the alarm, and she probably couldn't outrun him, but maybe she could lose him in the underbrush.

Until she remembered all the assorted cameras in and around the home and Rocky. She did not doubt he'd find her scent right away, making escape unlikely.

Plus, there was another reason not to run: She wanted to find out the truth about herself.

And if she had done all that they'd said, she was ready to pay the price for it.

The old Amanda might have been bad, but the new Amanda that had emerged after the blow to her head was not.

She was sure of that.

Armed with that conviction, she walked over to her bed and slipped beneath the covers.

Sleep wouldn't come easily, or be untroubled, but it would come eventually.

In the meantime, she'd fight to get to the truth about who she was so she could get on with her life.

With or without the intriguing police officer.

HE'D PLANNED ON RELAXING, maybe even catching a few hours of sleep on the sofa.

Their quarrel had made that virtually impossible.

Because of that, he snatched his laptop off the desk's surface and sat down on the couch to check on something he'd mentioned to Jackson earlier.

He typed in "acquired savant syndrome," hoping to find an explanation for Amanda's knowledge of warrants, escape techniques, and so many other little things.

But as he read through the many stories about sudden changes after head injuries, it occurred to him that those had been radical transformations. People who didn't play musical instruments instantly becoming gifted musicians. Same with people developing high-level artistic skills or the ability to play competitive-level chess.

Amanda's case didn't seem to reach that degree of change, and he suspected Jackson's cousin Ricky would likely confirm his conclusion.

Which meant that besides finding out who had taken Amanda from WITSEC, they had to find a way to restore her memory.

The meals they had shared had seemed to elicit memories.

Jumping back online, he dug through several articles on restoring memory, and it was no surprise that smell could instantly trigger emotional responses because smell, unlike the other senses, was more closely connected to the areas of the brain associated with emotion and memory.

Since her parents had been Mexican and Cuban, maybe serving her familiar foods might arouse lost recollections that could help with their investigation.

He'd had some Mexican and Cuban food on occasional dinner dates in Denver.

What he normally ate in and around Regina consisted of barbecue from their friend Declan's joint, burgers, or other meat-and-potato meals like his Irish mother made.

But the internet was a wondrous thing, he thought, as he searched for simple recipes he might be able to recreate to elicit recollections about Amanda's past. Maybe even her present.

Some were simple, like toasted Cuban bread with butter, served with Cuban coffee and a side of tropical fruits.

Others were more complex, like huevos rancheros, but even though they might be harder to make, he suspected the aroma of the fried eggs, warm salsa, and tortillas might be more triggering, hopefully in a good way.

Since Amanda—and he had to think of her as Amanda to keep up his guard against the tortured emotions he was feeling—had done most of the cooking so far, he set aside the computer and went to the fridge, wanting to see if they had the ingredients for breakfast.

Eggs. Check.

Jar of salsa. Probably not the tastiest, but there were peppers, onions, and garlic he could use to amp up the flavor.

No tortillas.

He opened the freezer to a pleasant surprise.

A frozen loaf of Cuban bread. Maybe not surprising since Jackson's cousins were half Cuban.

His mom, ever a saver because she'd grown up during difficult times in Ireland, had used to freeze leftover bread all the time. He knew just how to warm it up in the morning to use instead of the tortilla base that was traditional for huevos rancheros.

Feeling as if he'd accomplished something that might help in their investigation, he returned to the sofa and his previous plan for the night.

Grabbing a throw, he pulled it over him, and eyes half closed, he switched from the television to the laptop with the camera feeds. Likewise, he occasionally turned his attention to the noises outside.

The rustle of leaves as a spring storm kicked up.

The pitter-patter of rain on the roof and against the windows.

It was those natural sounds that pulled him into a half sleep that was shattered by the chiming of the alarm he'd set in the hopes of waking before Amanda did.

That way, he'd be able to make what would hopefully be a memory-inducing breakfast before they drove to the car rental facility at the airport.

Driving, which necessitated a car, he thought with a start.

Jackson had brought them here in Rhea's car, then left in it. Hopefully, he'd come back to get them and provide some kind of transportation. But just in case, he dashed off a quick text to Jackson about it, certain he'd already be up thanks to Axel's morning schedule.

His boss quickly confirmed he would be by in a couple of hours, and with that done, Mark turned to feeding Rocky, letting him out, and making breakfast.

He pulled an espresso maker from a cabinet, intending to make Cuban-style café con leche.

But first, he grabbed the ingredients for the salsa out of the fridge, along with the tray of eggs and frozen Cuban bread.

He loved to cook and made quick work of chopping the peppers, onions, and garlic and adding them to a frying pan with some olive oil. It didn't take long for the aromas from the vegetables to fill the air. While waiting for the veggies to soften, he defrosted the bread and, once it was ready, he'd toast it to act as the base of the eggs and salsa.

He had just added the salsa to the veggies when the sound of water in the pipes overhead said that Amanda was up and in the shower.

Good, he thought.

At a scratching sound at the back door, he opened it for Rocky to come back in and pushed on with making breakfast.

THE FAMILIAR SMELLS had teased her awake.

Memories came of her mother again, making them breakfast before they'd go to school. Her mother would sit with them at an old oak table, sipping her café con leche as she listened to them chat about all their friends and classmates.

Them, she thought. Not just her. Her sister, too.

Her mother's face came to her, the haziness fading and becoming a sharp image of a woman with long, dark brown hair and bright blue eyes framed by deep smile lines. An older version of herself, she thought as she rose and hurried to the mirror in the bathroom.

Yes, an older version of herself.

But that was where the recollections stopped.

She shook her head, forcing away sadness, and instead embraced joy at remembering her mother's face again.

Hurrying through her morning rituals, she dressed and joined Mark in the kitchen.

She walked up behind him, laid a hand on the small of his back, and inhaled the smells of her past.

"I remembered my mami this morning. I look like her."

He turned slightly and smiled. "She must have been a beautiful woman."

But then he shook his head and muttered, "Sorry. That was inappropriate given the circumstances."

Maybe, but she didn't mind. "Can I help?"

Jerking his head in the direction of the toaster oven, he said, "We don't have tortillas, but there's some bread in there you can slice and toast. Also, not an expert at using the espresso maker."

She chuckled. "Not a problem. I can handle both of those things."

It wasn't long before they were sitting at the table, eating the huevos rancheros, munching on toasted and buttered Cuban bread, and sipping sweet café con leche.

She dipped her bread in the coffee and then popped the sodden mess into her mouth.

"Mmm. I remember this. Toast and coffee were usually our breakfast," she said, and it suddenly occurred to her.

Motioning to all the foods and the coffee, she said, "You did this so I might get some memories back."

With a chagrined smile and a nod, he confessed. "I did. I'm sorry—"

She held her hand up like a cop directing traffic. "Manipulative, but don't apologize. I woke to a memory of my mom. A happy one."

His smile broadened, displaying a dimple on one side, and again it struck her that she loved men with dimples.

"I'm glad that it was happy," he said, and ate the last of his eggs and salsa. Raising his mug, he took a tentative sip, meeting her gaze over the edge of it as he said, "What about your sister? Anything there?"

With a sad shake of her head, she said, "No. Nothing. But if I look like my mom, she might also."

She fed Rocky the last little bite of her bread and then finished off her coffee. Just in time, as the front door opened and the sound of the alarm shattered the morning quiet.

Jackson walked in, locked up behind himself, and joined them at the table.

"Smells great," he said, eyeing the coffee almost enviously and prompting Mark to say, "Help yourself. There's more on the counter."

"Mark cooked it so I'd remember something, and I did. I saw my mom's face this morning. Remembered mornings with her. It was a nice thing," she said as Jackson poured himself some coffee.

"Good. Hopefully, that's a sign that more memories will start coming back soon. We should get to the station as soon as we can. CPS is sending one of their associates to check our cars to make sure there aren't any trackers on them," Jackson said, then sipped his coffee and glanced at his watch.

"Any other news?" Mark asked, and Jackson nodded.

"CPS confirmed your info on the rental car, and Ryder has a colleague who's worked with Rossi before. He's meeting with him this morning to learn more about the marshal. Maybe even get some other names about who's on Rossi's team."

"Sounds promising," she said, optimistic that they would soon get to the bottom of what was happening.

But what would that mean for her? A trial and jail? She fought that fear, reminding herself that whatever they discovered would prove she wasn't a criminal.

To allow the two men to chat more privately, she busied herself with cleaning the plates. Plus, she made a mental note to ask Mark if they could stop for more groceries or have someone get some for them.

The CPS home had been fairly well stocked with staples, but fresh cream, milk, and fruit would be welcome.

She started the dishwasher just as the men finished their huddle and motioned for her to follow them and Rocky outside.

Once there, Mark signaled Rocky to the back seat and harnessed him in. She hopped into the seat beside the canine while Jackson took the wheel and Mark sat in the passenger seat. He turned and handed her a cap with the Regina Police Department insignia and gestured for her to tuck her hair beneath the cap.

When she did so, he smiled and said, "Thanks."

It wasn't a long ride, but the tension grew as they left the CPS property. Both men were obviously on high alert, constantly checking the road, especially as they hopped on the highway for the very short trip to the police station.

"All clear so far," Mark advised, but as they neared the station, he said, "Duck down, Amanda. I see a black sedan with a man sitting in front of the police station. It's probably Rossi."

She did as he asked, hunkering down below the line of sight.

Jackson slowed before the turn into the police station parking lot. "Definitely Rossi," he said, and Mark grunted his agreement.

"Good to have eyes on him. He looks older than in his official photo," Mark said, and she stored that information for the future.

With a slight bump and incline of the car, they moved ahead, she assumed into the parking lot.

Once there, Jackson stopped the car and said, "Stay low. There's a car I don't recognize in the lot."

But a second later, Mark said, "They're wearing a CPS jacket. It must be the person here to check for trackers."

"Just wait until I confirm," Jackson said, and from her spot, she saw him leave Mark behind until it was clear she was safe.

He must have signaled Mark since, within a minute or so, Mark came to the back seat and unharnessed Rocky. As he did so, he said, "All clear, but please stay there for now. Rossi may decide to visit."

She did as he asked, even as her back complained from the awkward position. Long minutes seemed like forever until she heard the opening and closing of doors and the start of a powerful engine.

The sound neared, and suddenly Mark's voice came from a short distance. "It's safe to hop in."

She sat up.

He had parked his Jeep beside Rhea's car with the passenger seat aligned with his front seat. She transferred to his car and, as she'd done before, dipped down so Rossi wouldn't see her.

Chapter Fifteen

Mark wasn't going to tempt the devil by driving past where Rossi was sitting across from the police station.

There was an easement that ran into the police station parking lot from a nearby electric power station service center. Several homes lined the easement, which would block any sight of him taking that rough gravel path.

He did it slowly, trying to avoid the worst of the dips and divots on the rarely used route. Especially in light of Amanda's awkward position.

"Not much longer," he said, and a few minutes later, he pulled into the service center parking lot and was satisfied that there were no suspicious vehicles there.

"All clear," he advised, and Amanda immediately sat up.

"Thanks. I feel like I twisted myself into a pretzel down there," she said, and stretched. The motion gave him a too-tempting view of her breasts beneath the cotton of her blouse.

"We're good for now. Just keep an eye out for anything that seems out of the ordinary," he said as he fought down his response to her.

"Yes, sir. 10-4," she said with a small salute.

It hit him again that she was not responding the way a civilian would, making him think that this Amanda was not what she seemed.

It was obvious she was vigilant, as he was, on the drive, constantly checking the side-view mirror and occasionally pulling down the passenger seat visor to also look behind them. It kept their discussion to a minimum on the almost hour ride to the airport on the outskirts of Denver.

When they reached the rental facility, Mark parked the car and faced her. “Are you ready?”

“As ready as I’ll ever be,” she said, and for good measure, pulled the cap down slightly and lifted her jacket collar to obscure as much of her face as possible.

When she stepped out, Mark came around with Rocky, and they walked toward the small office for the rental facility. A bored-looking, early twentysomething manned the counter. He had been focused on his phone but looked up as they entered.

No wonder he’d been doom-scrolling, since there were no other customers in the place, unlike the other nearby businesses, which seemed relatively busy in comparison.

“How may I help you?” he said and stood. He was tall and gangly, like a puppy that still needed to grow into its body.

Mark pulled out his badge, and the young man’s eyes widened.

“Whoa,” he said with a murmur of worry.

“You rented this vehicle,” Mark said, and pulled up the photos from their security cameras.

The representative took a quick look and nodded. “Looks like one of ours. But don’t you need a warrant or something to get the name of who rented it?”

“No, we don’t need a warrant, but feel free to check with a manager—”

“I am the manager,” the young man said and puffed his chest out proudly.

And not all that smart, Mark thought.

But before he could say anything else, Amanda turned on the charm.

“That’s amazing for someone as young as you. Are you responsible for all the rentals that come in, Philip?" she asked, taking his name from the tag.

With a brilliant smile directed at Amanda, he said, "Most. I work the busiest days and nights. You can call me Phil."

"Because they trust you to do what's right. That's why I get why you wouldn't want to cooperate, but it would be really helpful if you could just look at some photos for us," she said, and wiggled her fingers for Mark to hand over his phone.

"Phil, we think this is the guy who rented that car. All you need to do is nod if it's him, and no one gets in trouble," she said and swiped to a photo of Rossi.

The "manager" shook his head. "Not him."

"Are you sure? He looks older now, Phil," she said, and did a second look at the photo herself before holding the phone up again to the young man.

"I'm sure. I remember the guy because he screamed either cop or military. Younger. Late thirties, maybe. Buzzed and neat," he said, and ran his hands across the sides of his head to demonstrate the haircut.

She was working him wonderfully, so Mark didn't interfere as she continued with her interrogation.

"You're very tall. Strong. As tall and strong as you?"

A vehement shake of his head provided an answer. "No, but at least six feet. Like bodybuilder muscles," he said, and mimicked someone flexing their arms. "Like I wouldn't want to get into a fight with him."

"Did you notice anything else? Tattoos? Scars?" she pressed.

Phil looked away, searching his memories. With a nod, he traced a spot on his upper arm with his index finger and said, "He had a T-shirt on, and there was part of a tattoo here. Red, like maybe the bottom of a heart."

"Awesome, Phil. You've been an amazing help. Can I get your number? Just in case we have some other photos, or I need to reach you," she said, her voice pitched low and almost seductive.

Mark understood better now how she might have swayed men to hand over their money. She was a good read of character and had known just how to play the young manager.

Philip grabbed one of his business cards, turned it over, and wrote down what he suspected was his personal cell phone number.

She smiled as she read what he'd written. "Thanks, Phil. You're the best," she said and then pushed away from the counter to exit the facility.

He followed, Rocky at his side. Once they were all settled in the car, he faced her.

"You were…amazing," he said, and yet she suspected it wasn't entirely a compliment. Beneath his appreciation of her skills she heard a hint of worry.

She got it. He probably thought she'd used those skills to con investors. In the back of her mind, a recollection crept in of her questioning someone, but not in a business office. More like a police interview room.

She stopped short with that memory, prompting him to stop and glance at her.

"Something wrong?" he asked, gaze narrowed as he examined her.

Because the memory was too new and slightly confusing, she shook her head and moved the discussion in a new direction.

"No, I was just thinking that just because he looked and sounded like a cop doesn't mean he's someone involved with Rossi."

"You're right. It could just be a coincidence or a hired gun," he said, but didn't believe that any more than she did.

As they started to walk again toward the car, Mark said,

"Let's assume it wasn't an innocent visit last night. How did they know where to go?"

"You're right. CPS is hypercareful about so many things. I doubt they'd have that house in either their personal or company name," she said and slipped into the passenger seat.

She waited for him to harness Rocky in the back seat, and once he was seated, resumed the discussion. "If they used a shell company, it would take some investigating, but you could connect the dots back to them. Same registered agent. Address. Things like that."

He examined her carefully yet again. "You seem to know a lot about how to do that."

She did. She didn't know why, and she wondered why Amanda would because she still refused to think of herself as the woman who had stolen from so many people.

It occurred to her then why Amanda would know.

With a shrug, she said, "Amanda probably used shell companies to shuffle the funds around and hide where the money went."

His lips thinned into a sharp, unhappy slash, and his features hardened. "Yes, that's probably how you did it."

He jammed the car into gear and almost peeled out of the parking spot, anger evident in every tight line of his body.

Anger at her, at Amanda. She did not doubt that.

But also anger at himself for what he was feeling. She did not doubt that, either. He had the same unwanted emotions for her that she had for him.

She admired his tenacity and intelligence. She admired his courage as a police officer who risked his life to protect others. And she'd seen the way he cared for Rocky. For her. It wasn't hard to imagine how caring and compassionate he'd be in a relationship.

But not until they figured out what was going on. That was first and foremost.

She had to know who she was and what she'd done before she could indulge her feelings for him.

Was his attraction as strong? she wondered during the long, tense, and silent ride back to Regina. But as they neared the turnoff for town, she noticed the Ford Fusion coming up fast on their tail.

"We've got company," she said, since the car was moving way too quickly toward them.

Mark glanced into the rearview mirror and nodded. "Looks like it," he said, then stepped on the gas and shifted into the left lane.

The Ford did the same shift, but kept two cars between them, as if they needed a screen to hide their approach.

MARK SCRUTINIZED THE Ford again in the rearview mirror. To get a better look at the driver, he shifted back into the right lane and slowed.

As the cars sped ahead in the left lane, he peered into his side-view mirror and thankfully had a clear look at the Ford.

The driver had on a baseball cap and sunglasses, making accurate facial recognition difficult. But he could make out a strong jawline and a stubbly beard.

Rossi had some slight jowls going on thanks to age, and had been clean-shaven that morning. He'd noticed that as they'd driven by him.

Definitely not Rossi, but if it wasn't, who was this driver, and why was he after them, or was it yet another coincidence?

Amanda looked out the window as the Ford sped by, but before they could get a good look at the plate, the car zipped off the highway on one of the few left exits on the route to Regina.

Amanda muttered a curse. "Was it him or just a quirk that it was the same make and color?"

"He fit the bill from what I could see. Right age. Buzz cut

hidden by that ball cap," Mark said, eyes scanning the road both ahead and behind to see if the car came back onto the road.

"What is it they say? Once is chance. Twice is coincidence. But three means we need to take action," she said, and counted down on her fingers in emphasis.

"You're not wrong," he said, thinking that too many things were coming together at the same time.

Because of that, he gave the car a voice command to call Jackson.

"How did it go?" his boss immediately asked.

"Not Rossi, according to the manager at the rental car facility. A younger man rented the car, and we think we picked up a tail just a few minutes ago. Same make and color as last night. Couldn't read the front plate," Mark advised, remaining vigilant for any sign of the Ford again or any other tail.

"How far are you?" Jackson asked.

"About ten miles away from the turnoff for the CPS safe house. Fifteen from you."

"Don't come here. Rossi is still sitting outside. But CPS has news for us on Rossi's team members. Let us know as soon as you're at the safe house so we can have a meeting," Jackson said.

"10-4, Jax. We'll call as soon as we're there," he said, but no sooner had he ended the call, he caught sight of another Ford Fusion in his rearview mirror.

No, not another, he thought. The same one as before.

"Hold on. He's back," Mark advised as he shifted lands and sped up.

He called Jackson again, and as his friend and boss answered, he said, "I need a BOLO on a black Ford Fusion. Use the plate numbers from last night's screenshots."

"He's back?" Jackson asked.

"He's on our tail again. Truth be told, he knows where we're going, but I'm worried that the last thing he wants is for us to get there," Mark said, hands tense on the wheel as he shifted in and out of the lanes, speeding to put distance between them and the Ford who was trying to match their every move.

"Don't go to the safe house. Head to my parents' place on the lake. I'm sending two squad cars in your direction to contain that tail."

"10-4," Mark confirmed and pushed on, swerving in and out of the light traffic on the road.

The turnoff for Jackson's parents' lake house was coming up quickly, but he could bypass it and backtrack to keep the driver of the Ford from determining their destination.

At one sharp turn, the Jeep rocked up on two wheels, its height and narrow wheelbase not ideal for such intense maneuvers.

"Mark," Amanda said, fear in her voice as he fought the wheel to regain control before they tipped.

The 4x4 came down hard, jerking the wheel almost free of his hands, but he somehow muscled the car under control again.

From the corner of his eye, he realized Amanda had braced her hands against the door and dash to stay safe.

"We're okay. We're okay," he said even as his heart pounded a fast, staccato rhythm.

He had to stay calm, he told himself, making another severe turn that rocked the car angrily and threatened to send them against the guardrail until he once again righted the 4x4.

Luckily, his actions managed to keep the Ford a good distance away, and as he looked forward, the flashing lights of two Regina squad cars approaching in the opposite lanes brought relief, as did the sight of an exit, just yards away.

He raced across the highway, cutting in front of a car in the right lane, earning a long blare of a horn. A heartbeat later, he flew onto the exit ramp.

Chapter Sixteen

The Ford, boxed in by a car to his right, shot past the exit.

She sucked in a breath of relief as they bounced and swerved onto the side road.

Especially as two squad cars zipped by them on the highway, giving chase to the Ford that had been tailing them.

"We're safe," she said and finally released her death grip on the door and dashboard.

"For now," Mark reminded, then slowed the Jeep and turned onto a side road.

"Is it far to Jax's parents' home?" she asked as she gazed at the woods around them that thinned as Mark detoured to another street that ran close to the lake.

"It's at the farthest part of the lake, past the spillway," he said and shot a quick glance at her. "It may only be a temporary stop. If they found the CPS location that quickly, they may be able to find this even faster."

Determination rose quickly inside her. "I'm not running anymore, Mark. If it's the marshals that find us, I'll go with them."

"And if it's not?" he challenged. "Do you really think either Jax or me would let someone hurt you?"

"I know you won't. But am I worth that risk?" she said, worried that whoever wanted her gone wouldn't hesitate to kill.

Something slipped over his features then, briefly, before he returned his attention to the road. His jaw muscles were tight, tense, as he said, "Yes, you are."

If she were the Amanda who had committed the fraud, she wasn't sure she deserved such loyalty.

She turned her attention to the landscape and the nearby lake, memorizing the route in case she had to make another escape.

It wasn't all that far to the house. Maybe fifteen minutes or so, even with their backtrack on the highway.

In no time, they exited the winding road and drove down a gravel-and-grass path to a spot close to the lake.

It was a sizable home in a rustic cabin style with a welcoming front porch that wrapped around the building. A long set of steps led to the generous porch that boasted two large rockers and, between them, a small circular table. It was easy to picture sitting there, enjoying the view of the lake on a warm summer night while sipping something icy cold.

A short, sloping path of spring green lawn led to the lakefront and was bisected by a pea gravel path that led to a walk along a small stream that fed the lake.

"Beautiful. But aren't his parents home?" she asked as he laid a hand on the small of her back, offering support as she climbed the steps to the front porch. Rocky loped ahead of them and sat by the front door, waiting for them.

"They go to Florida for the winter months and come back in mid-May, so it's empty for now. Jackson and Rhea visit regularly to keep things neat," he explained.

As she turned and caught sight of the lake, its surface glittering like diamonds beneath the brilliant sunlight of the late spring day, she didn't know if she would want to leave such beauty even in the winter.

But that moment of peace was shattered as he said, "We should get inside where it's safer."

He bent near the front door and removed a key from beneath a pot of pink primroses. She supposed the very feminine touch was courtesy of Rhea, and she hoped that one day she might be able to meet the woman who created such beautiful things.

The door swung into a comfortable open space area with a large sofa that faced a stone fireplace and a television. Opposite the sofa was an oak table big enough for at least ten and a kitchen that any cook would love.

A baby bouncer and a few scattered toys in one corner screamed *family* and brought a touch of heartache.

Would I ever have that? She fought the wave of sadness that swept over her.

Mark must have noticed something was amiss since he stopped and peered at her, face scrunched in puzzlement.

She gestured to the corner and said, "This is definitely a family place."

Mark smiled, almost wistfully. "It is. I've been up here when they do one of their big Sunday barbecues. It's a lot of fun."

But then he went into action, walking around the space with Rocky to make sure all the windows and entrances were secure. When he was done, they returned to the center of the living area. "There are two bedrooms in the back and one up in the loft," he said and pointed toward the ceiling.

She hadn't even noticed the stairs along one side of the room. Now, she followed them up to a large loft space that looked down onto the main living area and faced the lake. From that height, there was probably a clear view across the waters all the way to Regina.

"Time to call Jax and start that meeting," Mark said and dialed his boss.

When Jackson answered, he said, "I'll call CPS and have them send a video call invite to your email. Dad's laptop is on the desk. It's a new one I got him for Christmas when I upgraded their internet service. PIN is 0717. You should be good to go."

"10-4," Mark said, then hurried to the desk and laptop, and she met him there as he powered it up. Rocky had followed his master and lay by his feet, his massive mastiff head resting on equally huge paws.

After logging in, Mark opened his email and found the link, and a second later, they were staring at the faces of Robbie, Sophie, Jackson, and another handsome man she had not met before.

Sophie immediately introduced him. "Amanda, meet Ryder Hunt, my fiancé. He's with the Colorado Bureau of Investigation."

"I wish I could say it was nice to meet you, Agent Hunt," she said, given the nature of the circumstances for their introduction.

"Same, Amanda. But you're safe with us," he said, but she didn't miss the underlying tone in his voice.

"But not with the marshals?" she pressed.

"There's obviously been a problem with protecting you. My contact didn't know anything about this particular detail, but he seemed to have total confidence in Marshal Rossi," Ryder advised.

"But what about his team?" she said, impatient to know more.

"There are two or three marshals that Rossi has regularly had on his teams. I've got their names and photos, but I'm worried about your memory issues. So, I'm going to send them together with several other photos."

"Like a lineup," she replied.

"Like a lineup," Ryder confirmed with a dip of his head.

IT STRUCK MARK again that a regular person might not immediately think of a photo array as a lineup. Not unless they watched a lot of true crime shows or were familiar with police procedures.

But then again, Amanda had been arrested. She was probably well aware of that process.

A second later, a collection of about a dozen photos popped up on the screen. Similar looks for all the men in the pictures.

Fades and buzz cuts. Many sharply defined jaw lines and

muscled necks. Height was tough to tell from the headshots, but the build on some of the men was smaller.

A sharp breath from beside him snared his attention. "There's one that looks familiar," Amanda said and pointed at a photo in the rightmost spot of the bottom row.

"Are you sure? Let me blow that photo up for you," Ryder said, and the screen was immediately filled with the suspect's headshot.

Amanda leaned forward and her body shuddered, almost violently, as she softly said, "I know him."

"I have to ask again—are you sure?" Ryder said, tone patient and compassionate.

Amanda almost absentmindedly rubbed one wrist with a hand and did a wobbly nod. "Maybe. I don't know. I'm not really sure what I remember."

He didn't miss the look that Ryder shared with Robbie and Sophie as they sat at a table together.

"That's Marshal Mike Rogers. He's a regular on Rossi's team," Ryder advised.

"What do we know about him?" Jackson asked.

"I'll send over his CV in a second. For starters, he's been a marshal for at least six years. Military before that. Family man. Lives in the Denver area," Ryder said.

"Nothing out of the ordinary?" Mark pressed, thinking that there had to be something that would have the marshal suddenly join the other team.

"Nothing yet, but if it's there, we'll find it," Sophie assured them.

"What about Rossi? Do we ask him about Rogers?" Amanda asked while still nervously rubbing her wrists.

"I'll reach out to him. Won't take much since he's still planted in his car outside the station," Jackson said.

"In the meantime, we'll dig around and see what we find," Robbie said.

"I'll do the same here. We'll start by sending the photo to the rental car manager," Mark said, and shifted slightly to meet Amanda's gaze. She offered a small smile and nodded in agreement with the group's plan.

"Great. We'll meet again later tonight," Ryder said and ended the video call.

When he did so, Mark laid a hand on Amanda's, gently urging her to still the anxious motion.

"It's progress," he said, trying to alleviate her tension.

"And what if he is a marshal who wants me gone or dead, even?" she argued, and he understood. It was dangerous to downplay the possibility that Rogers was a traitor to his team.

"If he is dangerous, we'll find out and deal with him," Mark assured her and squeezed her hands to comfort her.

SHE TOOK SOLACE from that touch and deepened it, twining her fingers with his. But her brain was a whirlwind of images and questions—chief among them, Why?

"Why?" Mark said and dipped his head to examine her features.

She didn't realize she'd said it aloud, but now that she'd done so, she repeated it. "Why? For money? Revenge? You mentioned that Amanda stole from some retirement plans."

"You did, but I'm guessing someone was being paid to stop you from testifying. CPS will likely tackle that first, so let's start by sending the photo to that manager."

He downloaded the photo and handed her the phone. "Phil might be more receptive if he thinks you're calling him."

She didn't doubt that, and so she texted him, her tone friendly.

Hey, Phil. Remember me? she wrote, snapped off a selfie, and added it to the text just to make sure he knew she was reaching out.

Hey, you! Great to hear from you, he said and followed it with a few smiley emojis.

I was hoping you could help me out again. Is this the dude who rented the car? she said, added the photo, and ended the text with a smiley emoji.

A long silence followed, and she hoped she hadn't lost him with the question.

Dunno. Maybe. Can't be sure, bruh, he replied.

She showed Mark the response, and he blew out an exasperated breath. "Can you push?"

She could, but didn't think it would do much good.

Can you look again? It would really help me.

Another long pause followed, and she waited, breath held. Several seconds later, the little dots played across her screen, giving her hope he was responding.

The whoosh warning of a text sounded as his reply appeared on the screen.

Wish I could help, but not sure. Dudes like that all look alike to me.

Her body deflated with his response. She forced herself to type back a friendly response.

OK. Cool. Thanks, bruh. TTYL.

"So much for that," she said, and handed the phone back to Mark.

"It was worth a try. I'm going to look for anything public I can find out about Rogers," he said, and shifted the laptop around so he could work on it.

"I want to help. I'm good at seeing things," she said and motioned with her free hand to the computer.

He hesitated, clearly unsure about giving her access, but she pressed on. "You take the lead, and I'll watch. See what I pick up that you don't."

That seemed to mollify him. "Okay. Let's go," he said, and popped Rogers's name into the search engine.

ROSSI GLANCED AT the messages from his team members.

Williams had visited two locations yesterday tied to an assortment of shell companies they believed to be connected to Crooked Pass Security. Both had been vacant with no signs of any activity, but he had Williams checking in on them again today. Much like the day before, no activity.

Rogers had scoped out the last location the night before, but had been more optimistic about it being a hideout for their runaway. He had yet to report today, which worried him.

Had he been made? Was he possibly incapacitated? Or worse, had something happened with this daughter, again? he wondered.

Motion at the entrance to the police station drew his attention.

Police Chief Whitaker came down the steps and sauntered in his direction, a genial smile on his face. When he reached the car, he leaned his forearm on the roof, tipped his baseball cap back, and leaned in slightly through the open window.

"You must need to use the bathroom by now. Maybe have a coffee. You're welcome to come into the station if you want," the chief said, that smirk of a smile still on his features.

Impotent anger rose at the man's glibness, but he tamped it down. "Think you're smart?" he retorted.

"I think I'm smart enough to know that you don't know where Amanda Alonso is," he said, calmly and with little bite. "But I think both of us want the same thing."

"Which is?" Rossi said, brow arched in challenge.

"To get her back so she can testify. So, we can work together to achieve that or keep at loggerheads," Whitaker said, his tone all business.

The chief had tossed down a challenge, and as Rossi met the other man's sharp, gray gaze, it only confirmed he wasn't a man to mess with.

He wouldn't be the police chief at such a young age if he weren't sharp. And from all that Rossi had read of his military record, he'd been the best at whatever he did. It was time to have him as an ally and not an enemy.

"A cup of java sounds good right about now," Rossi said with a friendly tip of his head.

Whitaker stepped back to let him close the window and open the door.

They walked side by side to the door, where Whitaker held it open for him.

The desk sergeant's head popped up as they entered, and a slightly surprised look slipped across his features. But then he buzzed open the security gate, and Whitaker pushed through and led him to a small kitchen area at the back of the stationhouse.

"Help yourself. Doughnuts are fresh. We just brought them in for the afternoon shift," he said with a sweep of his hand in the direction of the coffee machine and a box that held an assortment of pastries.

"Don't mind if I do," he said, then made himself a coffee and grabbed a chocolate glazed doughnut.

After, he followed Whitaker to his office and sat before the other man's desk, setting his coffee there while he ate.

"Make yourself at home," the chief said facetiously.

"Thanks," Rossi said, wanting to be clear that he wasn't going to be bossed around by the younger man.

Once he finished, he grabbed his coffee, took a sip, and considered the chief over the rim of the mug. "How do you suppose that you can help me?"

"Alonso is missing. You think she's here, in Regina, I assume," he said, intelligent gray gaze narrowed as he awaited an answer.

"You know what they say about assuming," Rossi said, not quite ready to reveal his hand.

Whitaker let out a rough laugh, took off his baseball cap, and ran his hand across the longer strands of sandy brown hair. "So much for cooperation."

With a negligent shrug, Rossi said, "Why should I trust you?"

A long hesitation followed as Whitaker laid the cap on the desktop and leaned his elbows on the arms of his chair. He steepled his hands before his mouth and leaned back. Tipping his head to one side, he said, "Because I think you can trust me more than you can trust your team."

Rossi hated that the other man might be right. Ever since Alonso had disappeared, he'd had doubts about the reasons why. But Williams and Rogers were sticking to the story that she had taken off on her own because she'd had second thoughts about testifying.

"And what would you know about my team?" he asked, wondering just how much info the chief had been able to gather from his various sources, including the very well-connected Crooked Pass Security team.

"One of your team members is Mike Rogers. He's worked with you for several years already," Whitaker said.

"He has," he admitted, since the chief already knew that about Rogers.

Whitaker nodded, pulled over the file folder that Rossi had left him the day before, and opened it. He removed a photo and slipped it over the table for him to view.

Rogers's photo in a fake license. He forced himself not to react and handed the photo back to the police chief.

"Is there a problem?" he asked, although he worried about

how this small-town police department had somehow gotten that information and also why Rogers was using a false ID.

"Do your marshals normally speed around, driving dangerously, and use fake licenses?" Whitaker asked, eyes opened wide in emphasis.

"Do your beat cops normally interfere with marshals on an assignment?" he retorted, growing tired of the game they were playing.

Whitaker laughed and shook his head. Reaching over, he took the photo, slipped it into the folder, and then slowly closed it.

"I'd say we've reached an impasse, Marshal Rossi," he calmly said.

Rossi lumbered to his feet and pointed an index finger at the younger man. "Let me be clear, Whitaker. If you and your department are interfering with our investigation—"

"I thought it was just a protection assignment? Didn't know that needed an investigation," the other man said and rose, his greater height forcing Rossi to look up at him.

"Don't play games with me. If you know where Alonso is—"

"I'll be sure to give a call," Whitaker finished for him.

Rossi did not doubt that there would be no call coming, even though he was sure Whitaker knew where his missing witness was.

And he was going to have to find a way to get that info and get Alonso back in WITSEC custody before anyone else realized she was gone.

But as he walked out of Whitaker's office, he worried about Rogers and what his marshal was doing. It had been his carelessness that had allowed Alonso to escape in the first place.

If that was what really happened, the little voice in his head challenged.

Rossi had his doubts about Rogers's story. Alonso had been eager to flip on her old boss and boyfriend in exchange for a sweetheart of a deal. He couldn't see what would have suddenly changed her mind, but Rogers was certain that was the reason she'd fled while he'd been guarding her.

Rogers had always been an exceptional member of his team. But lately, Rogers had been distracted by his young daughter's illness.

Rossi had tried more than once to chat with him about it, but Rogers, ever the stoic warrior, had refused to open up, insisting everything was under control.

But what if it wasn't? Rossi wondered as he exited the police station and walked to the curb. He waited for a break in traffic and then crossed and slipped back into his car.

He took a moment to check his phone for any report from Rogers.

Nothing.

Blowing out a frustrated breath, he decided it was long past time to find out what was going on with his marshal.

Chapter Seventeen

Crooked Pass Security had assisted Mark and Amanda by granting them access to their heavy-duty facial recognition software. It had revealed several sites with old photos of Mike Rogers.

Quite a few of the hits were connected to his military service and volunteering with a few nonprofits dedicated to helping veterans. He regularly participated in fun runs and polar plunges to raise money for the various groups.

There were more hits on professional photos related to his time as a US marshal. Also, a couple of stories about how he'd saved the life of another marshal when they'd been attacked during an assignment, even though he'd been seriously wounded himself.

"He sounds like the kind of guy you'd want watching your back," Mark said as he finished reading one article.

Amanda leaned back in her chair, considering what they'd found so far. "He sounds like a real hero."

"You don't sound positive about that," he said, picking up the undertones in her voice.

She let out a long breath and shrugged. "The more I see his face, the more sure I am that he was the one who tied me up. Only..."

He scrutinized her for her hesitation. "Only what?"

With another, almost careless shrug, she said, "What if what I remember is when he took me into custody and not after, when he tried to hurt me?"

That possibility was something that he'd considered, as every hit on the marshal had portrayed him as an upstanding citizen.

But if Rogers hadn't been the one to take her, they were back to square one in their investigations.

"Let's assume he is the one who tried to hurt you since that's who you picked out, not Williams," he said, and gestured to the laptop screen.

"What could make a man like that betray his duty and dishonor his service?" Mark considered out loud.

SHE CONTEMPLATED HIS question intently, but with lots of reservations. After all, she had supposedly ignored her duty to all the people who'd given her money and now was about to snitch on her old boss and boyfriend.

That didn't make her a very good judge of character.

But inside came that push and pull again that said she wasn't that person. The thief and the rat. That she was an honorable person, even if that didn't jibe with everything she knew about herself so far.

The reason for Rogers's betrayal hit her then.

"He'd do it to protect someone he loves," she said and met Mark's gaze.

He held her gaze, possibly for too long, before a slow dip of his head confirmed his agreement. "He'd do it for someone he loves," he agreed and immediately returned his attention to the laptop.

"He's a family man, so let's start with finding out more about his family," Mark said.

Together, they searched for any sites that might have more personal information, but Rogers had been careful to lock down his social media sites. They were all set to private, and nothing in his profile provided any info about either a wife or children.

"The CPS file had his wife's name as well as that of his children," Amanda reminded him, but like Rogers, the wife's account was locked down, providing no information.

"Three kids, but all under thirteen," Mark said with a quick look at the file.

"I was twelve when I created my Facebook profile. I bet there are lots of tweens who lie to have one," she said, remembering how important it had been to her to be on the site and be able to see what was going on with so many of her friends who were also there.

"Rogers is a pretty common name, but let's give it a shot," he said and went straight to Facebook.

She laid a hand on his as he was about to start the search. "A tween isn't going to live on Facebook. It's going to be either Instagram or TikTok."

He executed the search on both sites, but all the hits were for older women.

Shaking her head, she said, "We've got to think like a girl tween. Try Sandy."

He did it with slightly better results, but no luck.

Muttering a curse, she closed her eyes and pictured how a young girl might present herself on social media. The answer came to her like a bolt of lightning.

"Try Sandz R."

His fingers flew over the keys, and bingo, there were profiles on both TikTok and Instagram that had possibilities.

"Thirteen. Home in Denver," she said, but if it was Rogers's daughter, she'd been careful not to share photos of her dad.

Mark eyed her carefully. "How did you come up with that?"

"Lots of contact with tween girls," she said, surprising herself with the revelation.

"How? Nothing in your file says that you had contact with tweens," he pressed, eyes narrowed as he examined her.

"Nothing in Amanda's file, you mean?" she said, feeling more and more distant from that person as she spent time with him. Especially as they sat there, working together. There was something familiar about that, and she was sure that wasn't something that Amanda regularly did.

"Stop, Amanda," he said and shook his head.

"That's not me, Mark. I know it isn't, but I can't tell you why I feel that way," she said, tapping a spot above her heart in emphasis.

He raked his fingers through his hair and snared her gaze with his. "This is a dangerous game you're playing."

"It's not a game, Mark. It's what I feel in here about me… and about you," she said and cradled his jaw. She ran her thumb across his lips, the touch intimate. A promise of what more they could have, but maybe it was a promise she couldn't keep if he was right about who she was.

She ripped her hand away and flipped it in the direction of the laptop.

"We should get back to work."

MARK DIDN'T ARGUE with her. Delving into the emotions they were both feeling could only cause problems.

Although the tween had been careful not to show her father in any of her photos, obviously well coached about the possible dangers of that, it seemed plausible that they'd found the right young girl.

"Go back to that montage," Amanda said and pointed to one of the videos the tween had posted.

He did, and as it played, Amanda shot forward in her seat and said, "There. Stop it there."

With the video paused, he hit a button to go full screen and then carefully reviewed the image. No matter how careful the tween had been, she'd inadvertently had her father in the background of one of the photos of the montage.

"Good catch," he said, surprised yet again by how observant she was. But then again, that was possibly one of the skills she'd used to con people.

He hit a few keys and took a screenshot of the video. "It's not real clear, but maybe CPS can enhance it and run it through their programs to confirm it's Rogers."

"And if it is, we may finally have a reason for why he might go rogue," she said, a deep frown marring her full lips.

"I imagine a father would do anything to help a sick child," he said, and hit the play button.

"Thank you all for watching and supporting my fundraising efforts. We're so close to reaching my goal," Sandra said, young face showing the signs of illness and the weight of uncertainty.

"It's so sad. She's so young," Amanda said, voice thick with emotion.

He wrapped an arm around her shoulder and hugged her hard. "She is young and that's a good thing. It seems as if this treatment would be perfect for her."

"Only if the insurance company would approve it, which they won't," she said, sadness shifting to anger.

"She's close to her goal," he said, but then tacked on, "But Rogers may have decided there was a quicker and more sure way of getting that money."

"If Amanda has money squirreled away, her boss likely did the same. If he did, he could pay Rogers to silence her and maybe avoid punishment."

He didn't call her on her dangerous game of denying that she was Amanda. There were more important things to do.

Replaying the video, he got a few more screenshots of the man in the background and then sent them to CPS so they could work their magic. He copied Jackson since he was also providing them the background on her illness, and sent along a link to Sandra's account so they could do their own review.

Satisfied with their work, he quickly looked at his phone.

"It's almost time for dinner," he said, and his stomach grumbled noisily as if to confirm it.

Amanda nodded and splayed a hand across her midsection. "I'm hungry, too, but I don't know what they have in their fridge."

"Hopefully food," Mark said and popped to his feet, but Amanda skimmed her hand across his forearm.

"I'll go check. I need a little time to think about all this," she said, and before he could stop her, she dashed off.

THE YOUNG GIRL'S story had touched her deeply.

Maybe because that memory of working with tweens had opened up a mental montage of young girls, many close to Sandra's age. And her gut told her that those girls had been facing obstacles of their own, much like she'd faced obstacles in her young life.

Which had her wondering what she really knew about herself. About Amanda, other than that she was a criminal who'd taken part in a massive financial fraud.

She vowed to find out more, but after dinner, she thought as her stomach growled to say, "Feed me."

The fridge section had some necessities. Butter. Half-and-half. Eggs. Several different cheeses. A bottle of chilled chardonnay.

Mark had mentioned that Jackson and his wife came up to take care of the place, and they likely took advantage of the fabulous location for some downtime.

The freezer had what she imagined physical men like Jackson and Mark would want: meat. Lots of it.

She pulled out some boneless rib eyes, her mouth watering as she did so.

Obviously, she was a meat-eater as well.

A search of a nearby pantry revealed onions and potatoes.

Great, she thought, and started dinner.

MARK TOSSED THE stick along the edges of the lake, and Rocky splashed through the shallow, cold waters to retrieve it.

He rubbed the dog's head and body, rewarding him before he repeated the throw, mindlessly doing it over and over as he processed the information they'd uncovered on Rogers's daughter.

If it *was* Rogers's daughter—although he was fairly certain that CPS would confirm it after enhancing the screenshots he'd sent them barely minutes earlier.

He was about to toss the stick again when Jackson's ringtone—"Enter Sandman"—blared across the quiet of early evening.

"Good work," his friend and boss said as soon as he answered.

"Thanks, but it was Amanda who spotted Rogers in that video. She's quite observant, and she's still insisting she's not Amanda," he advised, wanting to get it all out in the open.

"Head injuries can be tricky," Jackson offered in explanation.

"I guess. What do we do if CPS confirms it's Rogers in that video? Money is a prime motive for an assortment of crimes," he said, convinced that paying for his daughter's treatment would be a reason for the marshal to go rogue. Heck, in a similar situation, he might do the same.

"If CPS confirms, I'll reach out to Rossi. He came in today, by the way. I showed him that fake license Rogers used during the traffic stop," Jackson advised.

Mark had been surprised by that when his boss had sent him a photo of it earlier that day. "What did he have to say about it?"

"Not much. In fact, not much about anything other than to confirm they'd lost Alonso and we should stay out of their way," Jackson said, his irritation obvious.

"Too late for that. And I'd say we hold all the cards right now. We have Amanda, and we know Rogers was on the team. He had the opportunity to take her, and now we have a possible motive."

"All true, but I'd like to wait until CPS confirms before we bring Rossi in again. Do you think you're good for the night there?"

Mark did a slow perusal of the lakeside location and the large rustic-style cabin.

There were a few outdoor cameras on the house and a doorbell camera at the front door. The cameras and a basic off-the-shelf security system had been installed by Jackson a year earlier after a rash of break-ins at several vacation homes. Security was nothing like what had been available at the CPS safe house, but they still provided some measure of protection.

"I think so. I'll do a walk-around with Rocky to assess the situation better, but we'll be good for tonight."

"Great. CPS should have info for us in the next few hours. I'll call as soon as they do," Jackson said.

"10-4," he said and ended the call.

With a wave of his hand and a low whistle, he instructed Rocky to follow him and slowly surveilled the area in and around the house.

He walked up the drive to the narrow road off the highway that led to the property. All was quiet there, and as he ambled along the edge of the street, it was clear that anyone could stop there and work their way through the underbrush to the small backyard of the house.

Making a mental note to make sure to turn on the lights at the back of the home, he returned to the lakeside and down the pea gravel path to the area by the stream. Another problem. The stream was low enough that anyone could cross it from the adjacent property or farther upstream.

Glancing back at the house, he noted the one camera on the corner, but wasn't sure that would give him eyes on the stream.

Rocky nudged him with his massive head, and Mark reached down and rubbed his ears, rewarding him for his patience as they'd inspected the property.

A soft breeze swept by, bringing the aroma of roasting meat.

"I hope that's dinner," he said as he bent to give Rocky some love and attention.

Barely seconds later, the front door opened, and Amanda called out, "Dinner will be ready in a few."

With a wave, he acknowledged her and said, "I'll be there in a minute."

She smiled, returned his wave, and closed the door.

Such a homey exchange, and it was easy to picture it being a regular thing with her.

Until he reminded himself that she was a criminal and headed to jail.

Arming himself with that to battle his unwanted emotions, he rubbed Rocky's head and urged him to follow as he walked to the front door.

Chapter Eighteen

She lay on the couch, belly full from the dinner she'd made. Rubbing her stomach, she said, "If I must say so myself, those steaks were delicious."

Mark took a seat opposite her and laughed. "You did say it yourself, but yes, you're a great cook."

"I am," she said with a note of surprise. But then again, she seemed to be learning new things about herself constantly.

Except, of course, the really important things, like who wanted her gone, and why she had stolen hundreds of millions from innocent people.

But were they truly innocent? They must have known they were getting too good a deal, right?

She shut that dark side down of her mind immediately.

Stealing is always wrong, she thought.

"It is wrong," Mark said, surprising her. She must have lost control and said it out loud.

"I know it is," she said, but didn't push about not being that Amanda because he wasn't receptive to that argument.

Instead, she said, "What is the plan for tonight?"

"Another walk around the property to make sure it's secure and a call with CPS to see what they've been able to get from the photos we sent and any other information they've gotten."

"Mind if I come with? It's such a nice night out," she said, eager for a few more minutes of normalcy until reality returned.

He hesitated, prompting her to argue for her request. "If

Rogers wanted me dead, he could have done it already. I'm leaning toward the fact that he just wants me gone until it's too late to testify."

He nodded and slowly rose. "You're probably not wrong, but people have done awful things for the sake of family, including murder," he reminded.

True, she thought, and a niggling thought suddenly crept into her brain. *Aren't you doing this for family?*

This? Stealing?

Her parents were dead, and her sister…

Her sister's face still eluded her. Every time her sister popped into her memory, it was her own face that she saw.

Lost in those thoughts, she followed Mark and Rocky out the door as he said, "Let's go before it gets too dark."

They walked down the steps to the edge of the lake and then turned to do an amble up the driveway, both of them silent.

Was he thinking about what she'd said about Rogers? Or was he worrying about the fact that this location was nowhere near as secure as the one they'd left, but was no longer safe?

It wouldn't take Rogers long to find this property since it was probably in the Whitaker name, she thought.

But if Rogers came alone, Mark and Rocky were more than capable of handling him.

And if he didn't?

Her gut clenched with fear, but she told herself she could handle it. After all, she'd managed to escape, hadn't she?

They returned to the lakeside just as dusk fled, replaced by night.

The bright, glittering sunlit surface had become an almost watercolor drawing beneath the muted rays of a sliver of moon. In the distance, a dark shadow meandered along the surface. A cormorant, she was sure.

"It's so pretty here," she said and wrapped her arms around

herself as a slight chill had arrived with the coming of night. Her cotton T-shirt was no protection against the cold.

THE SHIVER THAT wracked her body communicated itself to him where their arms were lightly touching.

"Cold?" he asked, and at her nod, he drew her into his arms.

She fit there perfectly, her head tucking neatly beneath his jawline. All her soft bits matching his hard ones a little too well, like the missing pieces of a puzzle finally found.

He breathed in a contented sigh, and his senses were filled with her aroma, all fresh and flowery. Feminine.

As her arms slipped around his waist, he released his breath slowly, knowing he should end the embrace and yet loath to do so.

"This is so…wrong," he said, worried about where it might lead. Rocky seemed worried also as the dog butted his head against their legs, as if warning them to break apart.

"Funny, but it feels way too right," she said and peered up at him, blue eyes bright even in the dark of night.

A loud crunch and the snap of a branch had them jerkily jumping apart, but it was too late.

Two large bodies charged them, emerging from the woods in the stream area.

Masked men, gloved and dressed in all black, Mark noted as he swept his arm around and dragged Amanda behind him.

The man in the lead came at him, pausing within a few feet to snap open a police baton.

It would inflict a beating if he came near, but Mark wouldn't let that happen.

"*Packen, stell,*" he commanded in German, instructing Rocky to attack.

As he'd been trained to do, the dog leaped into action and went for the man's hand with the weapon. Powerful jaws snapped down hard, causing the man to cry out and drop the baton.

The man fell back, trying to free himself from Rocky's powerful jaws.

The second man had hesitated with the attack, but then flew at Mark, stun gun in his hand.

MARK HAD SWEPT her behind him, but as the men attacked, she fell back, not wanting to be in the way.

But as Mark battled not to be tased and the other man beat on Rocky's head, trying to break free, a desire to protect surged through her body, propelling her into action.

As the stun gun grazed Mark's forearm and his legs buckled, she kicked his assailant's knee.

The man groaned and whirled in her direction, intending to stun her, but she swiveled on one heel, avoiding the stun gun, and caught the man mid-chest with a kick.

Stumbling back with a look of surprise, the man delayed for only a second to come at them again while his partner continued to battle Rocky.

Mark, still weak from the tasing, staggered to defend her, and she joined him to fight off the attack, punching and kicking at the man.

She managed to dislodge the stun gun with another kick and was about to help Mark take the man down when a loud yelp of pain drew her attention to Rocky.

The second attacker had somehow picked up a rock and smashed it across Rocky's head, stunning the dog into releasing him.

When the man raised the rock for another blow, she rushed into action with a flying kick that landed squarely on the man's chest.

The man tumbled to the ground, and she drove her instep

against his wrist, hearing a satisfying crunch that made him drop the large rock and mutter a curse.

She stepped back, readied herself for his attack, all the while keeping an eye on Mark and his battle with the other assailant.

Mark landed a few good blows that drove the man to his knees, distracting her.

Suddenly, she was flying through the air and onto the lawn, the force of the other man's weight as he drove her into the ground stealing her breath. Her head hit hard on the grass, stunning her.

Black circles danced in her vision as she fought for a breath.

Mark called her name, as if from a distance, and Rocky's barking came from nearby.

The circles fled, leading her into darkness. Her last thought…

You're not going to die, Natalie.

IN ALL THE mayhem of the attack, Mark hadn't heard the ringing of his cell phone.

A good thing, he realized as the night erupted with the blare of sirens and flashing lights.

Their two assailants stopped dead in their tracks, and realizing that the cavalry would soon arrive, took off in the direction of the stream.

Mark was about to give chase when Amanda's loud groan registered above Rocky's barking and growling.

He was standing beside Amanda, protecting her.

She was lying on the ground, almost immobile except for her breathing and the slight, irregular twitch of her muscles.

He rushed over, kneeled close, and Rocky immediately ceased barking and growling, satisfied she was safe now that Mark was there.

"Good boy," he said and examined Amanda, trying to determine how badly she was hurt.

"Amanda? Amanda," he called out as her eyes fluttered open.

Her gaze was dazed as she raised a hand and brought it to her temple.

"Can you hear me?" he said, and as she struggled to rise, he eased an arm around her shoulders and helped her to a sitting position.

She shook her head, as if to clear it, and he asked again, more softly, "Can you hear me, Amanda?"

This time, the shake of her head was more definitive. "I'm not Amanda."

This again, he thought, but only for a hot second as she met his gaze, intense determination blazing from those amazing blue eyes. "I'm Natalie. Amanda's twin sister."

NATALIE NO LONGER had any doubt about who she was. It totally explained the few vague memories she'd had and why her sister's identity had been so confusing.

"I'm Natalie Alonso," she repeated, willing him to believe her.

He searched her features, puzzlement slowly becoming reluctant acceptance. "Okay. You're Natalie."

Red, white, and blue lights bounced across his features, and the sirens blared for a few seconds until they switched off as a police SUV jerked to a stop behind Mark's Jeep.

She was grateful for that since their screech had been hurting her head.

The police chief jumped from the SUV and rushed over. Seeing that she appeared hurt, he was immediately on his radio, requesting an EMT.

Mark helped her to her feet, her knees wobbly.

"Are you okay?" Jackson said, bending from his much greater height to examine her.

She cupped the back of her head, which was aching again from her impact with the ground. "I hit my head, and my ribs hurt. He pile-drove me into the ground. But I got my licks in. I think I broke his wrist."

Jackson nodded and peered at Mark. "What about you?"

Mark raised his arm to display a streak of red where the stun gun had grazed him. "Slight burn. Nothing serious, but Rocky may be hurt," he said, and released her to kneel and inspect his partner.

His fingers came away with blood as he touched the top of the mastiff's head, and he muttered a succinct curse.

"The big guy hit him with a rock. It's why I went to help. Rocky had him controlled until then," she explained, and likewise kneeled to check the dog.

The dog licked her face, as if grateful for her support.

It dragged a short laugh from her, but then the severity of the situation returned. She sluggishly stood, still a little unsteady from the attack.

Mark was instantly there, slipping an arm around her waist.

The action wasn't lost on Jackson, who raised an eyebrow at his sergeant's action. He flipped a hand in the direction of the house.

"Why don't we go inside to wait for the EMTs. I'm going to call in another unit to secure the scene and look for evidence," he said in a tone that didn't invite argument.

As he commanded, they hurried indoors. She took a seat on the couch, but Mark was all action, going to the freezer to make bags with ice for her and Rocky, and wetting towels for a quick cleanup.

He sat beside her and handed her the ice bag, which she immediately put on the lump at the back of her skull. That exposed her dirtied and skinned elbow, which he quickly tended to with the wet towel.

She offered him a thankful smile, and he turned his attention to Rocky, checking the dog's head and finding a small cut.

He used a clean towel for a further inspection and seemed satisfied it wasn't a serious injury.

"Want to tell me what happened?" Jackson asked as he stood before them, arms across his chest, clearly in chief mode.

"We were checking the grounds one last time when they rushed us from the stream area," Mark said, an embarrassed flush on his cheeks at having been surprised because she had distracted him.

Jackson raised a brow, but didn't push his friend and sergeant.

"It was my fault. I asked to go with Mark, but I was glad to be there to help him," she said, making that brow arch ever higher.

"Help him? How?" Jackson said.

"She can kick ass, Jax. She's obviously had martial arts training," Mark explained with an awkward glance in her direction.

"Amanda struck me as a bean counter, not a fighter," his friend countered, which gave her the perfect opportunity to repeat what she'd told Mark earlier.

"That's because I'm not Amanda Alonso. I'm her twin sister, Natalie. And I'm a Denver homicide detective."

Chapter Nineteen

Jackson grunted in disbelief, and Mark understood why his friend and boss was dubious.

"I get it, Jax. She's been denying that she's Amanda all along, but maybe we should hear her out," Mark said, wanting to make sure they didn't make a hasty and wrong decision.

With an exasperated and slightly weary sigh, Jackson waved a hand to urge her to proceed.

"About a month ago, my boss and I were approached by a higher-up at WITSEC. They weren't happy with the deals that the DOJ lawyers had agreed to because they worried that Amanda and her boss had hidden accounts with too much cash."

"Too much cash that could be used to silence someone?" Mark asked.

"Or help them escape. They didn't like either scenario, and worried that someone on the team might be susceptible to bribery," she explained.

"Rogers?" Jackson pressed.

With a shrug, Natalie said, "They weren't sure if it was Rogers, Williams, or even Rossi. That's where I came in."

"You took Amanda's place to find out who'd gone rogue," Mark said and wrapped an arm around her shoulders, believing her story.

Jackson wasn't so quick to accept her explanation. "I assume you have a name at Denver PD that can confirm your story?"

"I do. Just ask for Chief of Detectives Rick Warren," Natalie replied without hesitation.

A knock came at the door, and Mark rose, checked the door, and then let the EMTs in.

As the paramedics turned their attention to Natalie and Rocky, Jackson jerked his head to invite Mark to join him outside for a private discussion.

Once they were on the porch, Jackson looked back at Natalie. "She sounds convincing."

"I believe her," Mark said because her story had the ring of truth, and he'd seen firsthand how she had handled herself. A civilian wouldn't have reacted like that.

Jackson skewered him with his gray gaze. "Not sure you're being one hundred percent objective, Mark."

He couldn't deny it. "I have feelings for her. I can't deny that, and it's wrong. But it would be easy to confirm her story."

That seemed to bother his boss, and he understood why. "You're worried that if her boss and the WITSEC higher-ups find out her cover's blown, we'll never know which agent has gone rogue."

"I think it was Ben Franklin who said, 'Three may keep a secret, if two of them are dead.'"

"We have CPS working with us," Mark tossed out for consideration.

"CPS is family and, except for Ryder and his one contact, there is no connection to police brass or the Feds," Jackson reminded him.

"If we keep who she is secret, she's still a target, and Rogers and Rossi are still our top suspects," Mark said and glanced toward the lawn where the attack had taken place. An officer bent low to the ground by the lakeside and picked up what looked like a glove, which he placed into an evidence bag.

"Looks like Parker found something," he said and pointed

a finger at his fellow cop, one of the newer and younger members of the force.

Jackson nodded, and the two walked to join the beat cop. "What have you got there?" Jackson asked.

"Glove, and there's some blood on it," he said, and held up the evidence bag.

"Both men wore gloves, and Rocky bit one of them. Maybe the glove came off as the attacker tried to get free," Mark said as he recalled what had happened during the attack. Then he quickly tacked on, "And Nat… Amanda thinks she hurt his other wrist."

"Let's get that to the ME. I'll ask him to expedite getting what DNA he can so we can run it through CODIS that has all the samples of DNA from crime cases. I'll also get a call out to the local hospitals to let us know if anyone comes in with either a dog bite or broken wrist," Jackson said, and the young cop hurried up the driveway to the cruiser parked on the road.

As Mark watched him walk away, Jackson said, "I'll post a squad car on the road to keep watch. Do you think you can handle guarding her tonight?"

Mark drifted his gaze to the house and imagined the woman sitting inside with the EMTs. Recalled how she had handled herself when they had been attacked.

With a slow nod, he said, "I think the two of us can handle it."

Jackson had tracked his gaze, lips pursed in frustration. He was about to speak when his phone rang, and he looked down at the screen.

"CPS. It's time for our call."

THE EMTS HAD finished with her, confirming she had yet another light concussion from hitting her head. Again.

As the female EMT turned her attention to Rocky, cleaned and bandaged a small cut, her partner, an older man, said, "One concussion is bad enough. You've had two. You really should consider a trip to the hospital."

She waved him off. "I feel fine. Better than I did before."

Better because she remembered who she was and why she was impersonating her twin sister, Amanda.

The creak of the door signaled the return of Jackson and Mark.

Finished with Rocky, the female EMT packed up her bag, and then the two EMTs approached the cops. Jackson spoke to them in low tones and glanced in her direction.

The older man did the same and shook his head, muttering, "Stubborn."

But a second later, they were out the door, and the two cops joined her in the living room area. Mark sat beside her on the couch, and Jackson took a spot in a nearby recliner.

"CPS has some info for us. Are you up for a meeting?" Jackson asked.

"A slight headache, but otherwise okay. But what about the EMTs? Will they talk about what happened here?" she asked, worried that more and more holes were being poked through what little secrecy remained about this investigation.

"Mac—the older EMT—is an old friend. I asked him and his partner to memory-hole this visit," Jackson said.

She nodded and immediately regretted it as even that simple motion caused a wave of nausea to wash over her.

Mark must have noticed her discomfort since he stroked a hand across her shoulders and said, "Are you sure you're okay with this?"

"Yes-s-s-s," she almost hissed, eager to hear whatever CPS had to share.

"Okay. Let's see what's up," Jackson said and joined a video meeting. Sophie and Ryder were on one screen while Robbie was alone in another.

"First of all, we're sorry about what happened at our place.

We had given strict instructions to our lawyer about how to register that shell company to avoid any link to CPS, and he didn't follow our instructions," Sophie said, dismay obvious on her features.

"We've taken steps to make sure that doesn't happen again," Robbie added.

"No problem. We appreciate all you've done so far," Jackson said.

"We do have another location that we feel is secure," Sophie said with a glance at Robbie, who nodded in agreement.

Mark met Jackson's gaze and didn't need his boss to speak to know what he thought.

"We're not hiding or running anymore. They're going to need to come through all of us to get her," Mark said, deadly determination in his voice as he laid a hand on Natalie's leg.

"Yes, we're staying put," she confirmed, gaze locked with his.

"But we would appreciate anything you can do to help boost security at my parents' place," Jackson added, clearly aware that his cousins still had much greater resources than his small-town police department.

Sophie nodded. "We have your IP address from this feed. We'll see what other devices are using that address, and if it's a camera or other security device, we'll tap into them and have our associates monitor the feeds."

"We can also come up tomorrow and possibly add some things, like a driveway alarm at your parents' place," Robbie said.

"Thanks. That's appreciated," Mark said, grateful for their help.

"You said you had something for us?" Natalie said, and her attitude seemed to cause some confusion to the CPS crew.

"For us? Does it make sense to include a witness in our investigation?" Ryder asked, his features filled with concern.

"We have news for you also," Mark said, and Natalie immediately jumped in to repeat what she had earlier told them about her real identity.

Surprised silence filled the air for long moments until Ryder said, "You're saying they scrubbed not only everything about Amanda Alonso, but also you, her twin sister?"

There was no hiding his disbelief, Mark thought. He'd had his moments of doubt at first, but as he'd thought about it, so many things had pointed to her being someone involved in law enforcement.

"I believe her, Ryder," Mark said, conviction ringing in his tone.

"I do, too. I trust Mark's judgment," Jackson said, and Mark appreciated the support from his boss and friend.

Another long silence filled the air before Sophie said, "All right. But I'm sure you won't mind if we try to find out more about..."

"Natalie," Mark said.

"I'm a homicide detective in Denver," Natalie said with a dip of her head.

"We'll keep that to ourselves for now, I suppose?" Robbie said with an arch of a dark brow.

"Yes, keep it to us. In the meantime, could you get anything from those screen grabs we sent?" Mark asked, hoping that whatever they'd found would move their investigation along.

With a nod, Sophie provided their report. "We enhanced the photo, but it still wasn't clear enough to be one hundred percent certain. We ran it through John's predictive program, and it said there was an eighty-five percent chance it was Rogers in the background."

"We also ran all that we had on both Rogers and Rossi to ask it to calculate the possibility that either, or both, were involved in criminal behavior. Rogers beat out Rossi, seventy-five percent to fifty percent. We can send you the reasons the program made those calls," Robbie advised.

"Do you trust this program?" Natalie asked, clearly dubious about the results.

"We do. It's been incredibly accurate in our various investigations and in several police departments that are using it to identify possible crime victims and suspects," Sophie said, and Ryder chimed in with, "I've seen it in action, and it is amazing."

Her memory had come back to her in a tsunami of memories and images, although many still seemed fuzzy and out of focus. Especially those connected to her abduction from the WITSEC program.

But there was one solid thing: her detective's gut said to believe the CPS crew.

"I trust you, and hopefully we can get something from the evidence left behind today that will confirm the program's analysis," Natalie said and slipped her hand into Mark's. With a gentle squeeze, she confirmed she was good with the CPS info.

"What kind of evidence are we talking about?" Ryder asked, ever the practical Colorado Bureau of Investigation agent.

"Glove and blood. We're hoping to get DNA that we can run through CODIS," Jackson said.

"Can you get that analysis expedited?" Natalie asked, aware that such evidence would go to the CBI labs since a police department the size of Regina's wouldn't have the capabilities to process that kind of evidence.

Ryder nodded. "As soon as your local ME sends it to us, I'll have it expedited," he confirmed.

"Great. I'll make sure you have it tonight," Jackson said, determined to move the investigation along quickly.

"We're also putting a call in to local hospitals to watch for anyone with dog bites or a broken arm," Mark added.

"I'll do the same at my end in case they come in this direction," Ryder said.

"Great, I guess that's it," Jackson said, and after they all echoed their agreement, they ended the call.

Natalie sat back on the sofa, feeling relieved for the first time in days. She finally had her memory back and trusted that Mark, Jackson, and the CPS crew would keep her safe until they could confirm who was trying to keep Amanda from testifying.

But it would be a long night until they had something from either CPS or the evidence that had been gathered after the attack.

"I feel like I should be doing more," she said, impatient now that there were so many things she remembered, including why she was undercover in the first place.

Mark squeezed her hand, offering comfort as he said, "Remembering why you're here has already been a big help."

"But we still don't know if it's Rogers or Rossi or another agent who wants to stop Amanda from testifying," she said.

"It's interesting you still think it's just to stop Amanda and not kill her," Jackson said, picking up on her language.

With a shrug, she said, "He could have killed me when he took me. Or even done it tonight when they surprised us, but they didn't."

"Not yet, but he's getting more desperate. Do you know when Amanda was supposed to testify?" Mark asked, scrutinizing her features as she tried to recall what she'd been told.

But that information didn't come to her. "I can't remember. A lot of new things seem…fuzzy. Missing. Why can't I remember those?"

With a shrug and shake of his head, Jackson said, "Brain injuries are tricky. I reached out to my psychologist cousin Ricky for info, but he's out of town. Still, I'm sure he'll say the same thing. No one quite understands it, but it's not uncommon to forget things that happened in and around the time you're injured."

She supposed so, but once Jackson was gone, she intended to do some research of her own into that, as well as Rogers and Rossi.

As if sensing she was done with the discussion, Jackson popped to his feet. "Time for me to go. I'll check with the officers outside and make sure we have eyes on the road and lakeside and goose the ME to get the evidence to Ryder."

Together, Mark and she rose and walked Jackson to the door. No more secretive chats between the two men.

She was part of the team now.

"Try to get some rest tonight. I suspect tomorrow will be a busy day," Jackson said, then shook Mark's hand and hugged her.

"We will," she said, although she suspected both Mark and she intended to do a lot more work tonight.

As she cast a side-eyed glance at Mark, the little voice in her head said, *Not just work, Natalie.*

Chapter Twenty

The door closed behind Jackson, and Mark examined her carefully. "Are you sure you're okay? You took another hard hit."

She did the tiniest head bobble, as if testing herself, and then said, "A little wobbly, but I can deal. How's Rocky?"

His partner had been sitting close to him, head almost in his lap as Mark rubbed it, mindful of the bandage the EMT had put in place. He examined the dog, who peered at him with dark, somber eyes. "You okay, Rock?" he said and earned a long lick of his hand, confirming that his partner didn't seem to have any lingering effects from the blow to his head.

Meeting her gaze, eyes a stormy blue with her worry, he said, "He's good."

With a quick nod and a wince, as if the motion had pained her, she said, "Would you mind lending me a computer? I'd like to research some things."

"We can work together, if it's not an issue," he said, unsure of whether she was physically ready to jump into things, but she misread his reticence.

"Don't trust me yet?" she challenged, facing him, her gaze direct.

"I have no hesitation about trusting you. It's just that you should get some rest after another concussion," he said, worried she might be overdoing it with all that had just happened.

That mollified her. With a tight smile, she made a little cross over her heart and said, "I promise that if I'm not feeling well, I'll stop."

He could continue to argue with her but suspected it wouldn't do any good.

"Feel free to use the laptop. I'll make some coffee since I suspect it's going to be a late night," he said and went to rise, but she laid a gentle hand on his arm to stop him.

"Thank you for believing me," she said, voice husky with emotion, a ghost of a smile on her face.

She stirred him in ways that weren't wise, and yet he was hard-pressed to deny what he was feeling.

He cradled her cheek, his touch tender. Comforting. "Nothing about this has been straightforward, but together we'll figure it out."

Her smile broadened. "Together," she said, and cupped her hand over his, and for a long moment they just sat there, the moment deeply intimate.

But then he had to move because otherwise they might do something they both would regret in the morning.

It was too soon. Too soon, he told himself as he bolted for the kitchen to start the coffee.

NATALIE SUCKED IN a deep breath, battling the surge of emotions threatening to overwhelm her.

It was the concussion, she told herself. It was why she was feeling so…vulnerable. Needy. Overly sensitized.

This wasn't her normal self. She was pragmatic. Strong. Levelheaded. A tough cookie, her commanding officer had once said.

But she was feeling anything like that, maybe because Mark touched her in ways that no one else ever had before. She didn't know why.

For the last six years, ever since graduating from college and entering the police academy, she'd been surrounded by men like Mark and Jackson.

Alpha males. Honorable men. More than her share of handsome ones.

None had ever touched her like Mark, both physically and emotionally, she thought as she looked in his direction, watching as he prepped the coffeemaker.

Even when he'd thought she was Amanda, he'd been gentle and protective in unexpected ways.

And now that she was Natalie…

She hopped up from the sofa and snatched the laptop off the coffee table.

After walking to the kitchen table, she placed the computer so that he could see the screen as she worked. Even though he'd said he trusted her, she wanted to prove to him that he could. That there wasn't any reason not to believe her.

She powered up the laptop for her first search: finding out if the loss of more recent memories was common.

Her first results had just appeared when the earthy aroma of coffee filled the air. She had barely opened the first link when Mark placed a mug with coffee, black, by her hand.

"Thank you," she said and wrapped her hands around the mug, the warmth welcome.

He sat beside her, and Rocky followed him over. The dog lay down at Mark's feet as Mark sipped his coffee and took a quick look at the screen.

"Anterograde amnesia?" he asked, considering the results of her search.

She nodded. "It seems as if it's possible to have both anterograde and retrograde amnesia. No new memories versus a slow or gradual recovery. The former is rare, but I'm not feeling so positive," she said with a harsh laugh.

Slipping an arm around her shoulders, he offered a reassuring squeeze. "Just like your older memories came back, the newer ones may, too. It might take time."

"Time we don't have," she warned, aware that whoever had kidnapped her had to be as determined to stop Amanda from testifying as she was to regain her memories of the abduction.

"I don't know when Rogers was tying me up. Was it when I was brought into WITSEC or later, when someone took me?" she said, frustrated by her inability to discern the difference.

"But you don't remember Rossi doing that?" he said, trying to help her.

She shrugged, unsure, and closed her eyes, trying to replay what little she recalled on her closed lids. But although she could picture Rossi's face on that screen, nothing else came to her.

Opening her eyes, she did another little lift and drop of her shoulders, disgusted with herself. "No, I don't. To be honest, I can see Rossi, but nothing else about him."

"Do you think we can eliminate him as a suspect?" Mark said, tilting his head to watch her reaction.

She pursed her lips, considering it. "Maybe. Rogers has a stronger motive—saving his daughter. What's Rossi's motive?"

"His retirement fund lost tens of millions of dollars. Money is a big motive, especially if Rossi thought Amanda could make him whole again," Mark proposed.

Amanda had hidden money away, although her sister wouldn't admit it, not even when she'd spoken to her after her arrest. Natalie was sure of it, especially since Amanda had hired a high-priced shark from Denver. That took money.

Once Amanda testified and served her short eighteen-month sentence, she could skip the country and live off the millions tucked away in some Cayman Islands account.

"I don't understand why she did this. We were so close at one time," Natalie said with a sad shake of her head.

"Did something change?" he asked, then squeezed her close and tucked his head next to hers.

"Our parents raised us to be good people, and we were. In high school, we were like this," she said, and crossed her fingers in emphasis before continuing. "Then we split up to go to school. She wanted to be an actress. I wanted to be a cop."

"You're beautiful enough to be an actress," he said and brushed back a wavy lock of hair that had spilled forward.

HE SHOULDN'T HAVE said that, but once the words were out, it was too late.

A wry smile graced her lips. "Thanks. You're not too bad yourself."

He was grateful for the touch of humor in her voice since it helped tamp down the awkwardness of his statement.

"Did she change plans during college? Decide to do something else?" he asked, wondering at what had happened.

With another shrug and bobble of her head, she said, "Our parents were killed in an automobile accident during senior year. It was hard on both of us, but maybe more so on Amanda. She felt that it was so unfair, and it was, only..."

She stopped then, her voice thick with emotion. Her body tense beneath his arm before she relaxed and plowed on.

"She was mad at everything. Everyone, even me. But when she started dating Dave Peterson, she seemed to get better. I was glad she'd found someone who could make her happy," she said, turned her face a little, and met his gaze.

"He was older, handsome, and had lots of money. But more importantly, he treated Amanda well and made her happy. That was all that mattered to me, but I was so wrong about him," she explained, clearly wishing for him to understand, as if she had done something wrong by not realizing the kind of man Peterson was.

Rocky, as if sensing her upset, shifted from his spot at Mark's feet and sat by her, his mammoth head on her lap, offering comfort.

She rubbed his head, mindful of the small, glaringly white bandage. “Thank you, Rocky.”

“When did Amanda decide not to go into acting?” he pondered, since that had been her original goal.

“Peterson was older and had just started the venture fund when Amanda graduated. He needed help to get it going, and Amanda didn’t have a job. She fell into being his assistant while auditioning, and then gradually, she became more and more involved with the fund,” Natalie explained.

“The file we had said she was the chief financial officer,” Mark said, thinking it a leap to go from acting to becoming a CFO.

Natalie nodded. “Amanda is very smart. She caught on quickly on how to work with the customers and invest the money in an assortment of start-ups.”

Mark paused, lips tight until he exhaled a slow breath, as if unsure of how she would react to his next question. “You never got a sense things were hinky? That these supposed ‘start-ups’ were really shell companies that Peterson or Amanda had set up?” he said, emphasizing his words with air quotes.

She hesitated, still feeling some measure of loyalty to her sister despite what Amanda had done. “I was busy with my career. Plus, we always teased each other that I’m the older twin, but Amanda sometimes resented if I offered advice, especially after our parents died. She told me more than once that she didn’t need another mother.”

“It sounds like you drifted apart,” he said, sympathy ringing in his tone.

She hated to admit it, but they had. “We did, and I couldn’t find a way to reach her, especially with the kind of life she was leading with Peterson.”

FROM WHAT HE remembered from their investigation, Amanda and Dave had become almost celebrities, hobnobbing with the rich and famous, and donating millions to several politicians and political PACs. Possibly to have friends in high places if their fraud was discovered. Which made him think of something else.

"Where is Amanda?"

Natalie shook her head. "I don't know. My commander and the federal prosecutor are probably the only ones who have that info."

Since it didn't matter to what was going on with them at the moment, he said, "Let's review the reports from CPS to see how their program got those results. Maybe it'll trigger a recollection."

With a nod, they sat together, plowing through the pages and the various parameters that the predictive program had considered when deciding whether Rossi or Rogers was the more likely suspect.

As they flipped the last page, Mark leaned back and said, "It makes sense, but I didn't need a computer to tell me what's important. Family tops money every time."

"I guess it does. Only… Amanda put money ahead of me. Ahead of everything she'd ever been taught by our parents," Natalie said, shoulders sagging with her sadness.

He laid his hands across them, pulled her closer, and cupped her jaw to gently urge her face upward. "People make mistakes. Maybe Amanda regrets what she did."

"Maybe. Tough to know since I can't see her and who knows what'll happen once she finishes her sentence and takes off," Natalie replied, her gaze shimmering with unshed tears.

As one finally escaped and slipped down her cheek, he swiped his thumb across it, offering solace to her battered soul. "You'll find a way to talk to her. You strike me as the kind of woman who knows how to get what she wants."

Her gaze locked with his, and he did not fail to see the need there. But he also knew that she was emotionally raw and in a place that made her vulnerable.

"I can't deny I feel something for you, even when I thought you were Amanda. It was confusing for me, but now I think it's because I saw the real you, deep inside," he said and stroked her cheek again.

"I feel something, too, Mark. And as wrong as it might be at a time like this… I don't want to miss the chance to explore what we're feeling."

Chapter Twenty-One

She didn't wait for his approval or denial.

She swept close and kissed him, needing to feel alive again. Needing to feel his goodness chase away the doubt, hurt, and confusion that had filled her brain during this investigation.

He was stock-still at first, stunned by the kiss and maybe fighting what he really wanted.

But as she moved her lips against his, he slipped his hand to tangle in her hair and opened his mouth to hers, meeting her kiss. Tasting her, the kiss deepening until their breaths stuttered shakily, breaking them apart.

She sucked in a deep breath to calm her racing heart and the clenching of her body deep inside that said she wanted more. "I'm not sorry for that," she said.

A half grin awakened that tempting dimple as he said, "Like I said, you know how to get what you want."

"I want you… I think. It's so confusing…and weird right now. But I don't want to be alone tonight," she said, then rose and held her hand out to him.

INSANITY. RECKLESSNESS. IT would be professional suicide and a total lack of honor to give in when she was in such a susceptible state.

"I want, believe me, I do. But not now."

Her hand dropped like a stone, and her blue gaze turned the gray of storm clouds over the lake outside.

"I understand," she said, even though it was clear from her face and posture that she didn't.

That was confirmed as she raced away, and the slam of her bedroom door filled the night just seconds later, causing Rocky to jump up and bark.

"Easy, boy. It's all right," he said, and his partner settled back down.

But he couldn't be so settled. It took all his willpower not to go after her.

But somehow he didn't.

Instead, he sat there, mindlessly skimming through the pages of the CPS analysis again. As he had thought before, he didn't need a computer to tell him that family always won out over money.

That was why Rogers was the more likely suspect in Amanda's…no, not Amanda, in Natalie's abduction and all that had followed to keep her from testifying.

If he were in Rogers's shoes, he'd do whatever it took to raise the money for his daughter's lifesaving treatment.

But if it was Rogers, could they trust Rossi with the truth about his "witness"? Could Rossi help them bring in Rogers and end the threat to Natalie?

Shoving away the papers, frustrated by always being a step behind, he surged to his feet to head to the couch for the night. But first, a walk around the property with Rocky. His partner needed to relieve himself and the activity, and he needed to make sure someone had eyes on the area.

With a click of his tongue, Rocky sat up.

"Let's go, boy," he said, and together they walked to the door.

After dealing with the alarm, they hurried out onto the porch and then down to the lakeside, where he let Rocky nose along the shore and then near the house.

As he did so, a shadow passed along one side of the house. Rocky immediately whirled in that direction, growling and barking. Mark reached for his weapon until a spotlight snapped on, illuminating the figure.

"*Setz*," he said, commanding the dog to sit as he recognized his fellow officer.

"Parker. How's it going?" he called out and waved.

Parker returned the greeting and approached slowly, gaze on the large dog as a low growl escaped him.

Mark repeated the command and instructed Rocky to lie down. "*Platz*," he said, commanding the dog into the submissive position to calm Parker's reservations.

With what sounded like an annoyed huff, Rocky responded and lay at Mark's feet.

Parker came closer then and tossed a thumb in the direction he'd come from. "Just patrolling the grounds. Chief asked us to do it regularly. Adams is up in the squad car," he advised.

"Great. I'm just taking Rocky for a walk and scoping out the property myself."

Parker once again pointed back toward the side of the house. "A lot of underbrush there. They'd sound like a moose crashing through that. Easier to come across the stream," the young officer said, and jerked a thumb in that direction.

"That's how they did it, so keep a sharp eye in that direction," he advised.

"10-4," Parker said and ambled up the drive, his flashlight's beam bouncing back and forth as he searched the area in and around the property. Spotlights snapped on, bathing him in light and giving Mark some sense of peace, despite the earlier infiltration.

Which reminded him to ask CPS in the morning to find a way to secure that area.

With a hand signal, he sent Rocky in motion ahead of him, sniffing and dodging around the edges of the home and the underbrush.

At one spot, the dog paused and relieved himself, and once

Rocky was done, and Mark was satisfied his colleagues were in position, he sauntered back to the house.

A light snapped off in a back room. Natalie's bedroom.

The cabin was built on stilts, probably in case of flooding, not that it had happened in recent years, thanks to the spillway that had been built a decade earlier.

That put the bedroom a story up, which gave him a little relief since it would be harder to breach. Plus, there was a spotlight on the corner of the house that would discourage someone, lights being one of the best ways you could safeguard your house.

Too many people didn't take that most basic step, he thought, and hurried back to the house, stopping only to take a long look in the direction of the stream area once they were on the porch.

Satisfied all was quiet, he entered, reset the alarm, and went to the couch, Rocky at his side.

He'd dropped his knapsack there earlier, and he reached inside and took out a treat for his partner. Rocky eagerly grabbed the well-deserved bully stick, and as the dog happily mauled the length of dried beef, Mark lifted the bandage to once again examine the cut.

Minor, but there was some slight swelling. Luckily, Rocky was acting normally, relieving his worry about the injury.

One source of relief, while another worry still loomed large: Natalie.

He was worried about her safety, and not just from Rogers and his accomplice from earlier that night.

SHE'D JUST BEEN drifting off when a stream of light escaped from the sides of the blinds on the nearest window.

Hopping to her feet, she noticed the police officer walking up the driveway, the beam of his flashlight bouncing along the ground. In the distance, the steady flash of red, blue, and white lights warned that the property was being guarded.

Returning to the bed, she sat on the edge of it, all traces of sleep gone.

She debated slipping back under the sheets and trying to force sleep, but that would be a waste of time.

Grabbing a sweatshirt she had worn earlier, she slipped it on over the lightweight T-shirt she was using as a pajama top. There was a slight chill in the air, and she'd be too exposed in the thin T-shirt.

She entered the open-concept space and found Mark and Rocky lounging on the sofa in the living room area.

Arms wrapped around herself, bare feet chilly on the wooden floor, she ambled over, unsure of what her welcome would be.

He had the remote in hand and was just about to turn on the television when he froze as he saw her.

"I can't sleep. I thought I'd watch some TV in the hopes it might help," she said, but didn't move, certain he might not want her there. With him.

"Sure," he said reluctantly, then flipped on the television and grabbed a throw from the back of the couch. "You might need this. It's a little chilly."

She walked over and sat on the couch, but he was immediately in action. "I think I'll start a fire to chase away the cold."

Logs had already been set in the fireplace, and Mark tucked in some kindling, opened the flue, and lit the kindling.

He squatted there, waiting until the first wisps of smoke and the glow of a flame erupted from the pile of logs. Then he closed the fireplace screen curtain and returned to the sofa, choosing the spot farthest from the corner where she had snuggled into the comfy cushions.

The fire caught quickly, the aroma of a wood fire and its crackle and pop an accompaniment to the soft sounds of the television.

He handed her the remote. "Put on whatever you want."

She didn't really want to watch anything in particular. She was more interested in the man sitting across from her.

"What made you become a cop?" she asked, gaze narrowed as she focused on his features.

A slight lift of his shoulders was followed by, "I did a short stint in the army after high school. I decided I didn't want a military career, but I did want to serve the public. Regina PD was hiring. They would not only arrange for me to attend a police academy, but they'd pay me a salary as I did it."

"That's very generous for a small-town police department," Natalie said. She'd been paid as a recruit for Denver PD, but that wasn't unusual with a city as large as Denver.

"The old police chief, Bill Robinson, wanted Regina to have the best police department possible. Jax is continuing that with help from Crooked Pass Security."

She did not doubt it. Despite everything that had happened so far, the two men and their colleagues had been sharp and handled everything well. Still, it bothered her that all three safe houses had been compromised so quickly.

"How do you think they found us so fast?" she asked, laying her head on the back rim of the couch as drowsiness settled in from the heat of the fire, the comfy couch cushions, plush throw, and the peace and security brought by the man across from her.

"Not trackers. We checked for those, but both Rogers and Rossi have access to huge amounts of data as part of WITSEC. And CPS's lawyer seems to have messed up," Mark said.

Staring up at the vaulted ceiling with its large, hand-hewn beams, she said, "I hate being a step behind."

"I'm not a fan, either. But I feel like we're close, and once that DNA evidence is processed, we may have what we need."

The cushions on the couch shifted as he rose, walked to the fireplace, and jabbed the logs with a poker, rearranging them to keep the fire going. But he didn't add more wood, probably wanting to let the fire ebb if they'd both be asleep soon.

When he came back, he went to a comfy recliner right near her head, and Rocky sprawled on the floor nearby. As he pushed back to stretch out, he said, "Why did you become a cop?"

She glanced over at him, and with his position in the chair, they were nearly face-to-face. His green gaze was inquisitive, alive as it skipped over her features.

"My father was a police officer, but I saw how hard it was on my mother. The late nights and worry. But when my parents were killed, and those officers came to the door, they were so kind. And after, during the investigation, it reminded me why police are so important," she said, slightly choked up by the memories of that fateful day and all that had followed.

He cupped her cheek, offering solace with that simple touch. "I know you've probably heard this many times, but I'm so sorry for your loss."

"Thank you. It's funny but it both hurts and helps to hear that, even after so long," she said with a half smile, conflicted by that seesaw of emotions.

"Is being a cop why you knew so much about tweens?"

"Kind of. I volunteer at a local shelter for youth at risk. Part of our outreach to improve relationships between police and the community," she explained.

"Sounds like a good program."

She murmured a sleepy, "It is."

With the barest tilt of his head to peer in her direction, he said, "We should try to get some rest, but wouldn't you be more comfortable in bed?"

She shook her head vehemently. "I don't want to be alone."

Chapter Twenty-Two

Mark could imagine why.

It was hard to sleep knowing someone might attack at any moment.

But he was sure that after today's fight, they wouldn't try again tonight. They knew that both Natalie and he could hold their own against them, and adding Rocky to the mix decidedly made it a losing proposition. And now they had backup with the addition of the two police officers guarding the property.

"I think we're safe for tonight," he said, and she hesitantly nodded.

"Maybe. But when morning comes, I want to turn the tables. I want us to be the hunters instead of the hunted," she said, blue eyes blazing ice-cold fire.

"I'm sure we'll have more credible information that will let us do that. But we need to be fresh," he said, starting to feel the effects of the fight and too little sleep.

"Agreed," she said, then raised the remote and flipped to a station playing reruns of 1990s sitcoms that had become classics.

With the volume set low, he could still hear what was happening outside. A breeze kicked up, and tree leaves whispered in the night. Rocky raised his head, hearing the noise as well.

Seconds later, the patter of raindrops registered on the roof and against the windows.

"Just a storm, Rocky," he said and, with a hand command, urged his partner to lie down and relax.

"I love the sounds of a good storm and the smells," she said wistfully.

"Me, too," he said and reached for her hand.

He twined his fingers with hers, enjoying the peaceful time with the musical sound of the rain, the low murmur of the voices on the sitcom, and the fresh scent of rain as it drifted into the home.

Because of that peacefulness, he knew exactly when she fell asleep as her hand grew lax in his.

He allowed himself to relax then also, closing his eyes and slipping into a light sleep, confident in his colleagues outside and Rocky at his feet.

He did not doubt the canine would both alert and protect if anyone tried to enter the home.

He wasn't wrong as Rocky shot to his feet and raced to the front door, barking and growling. Teeth bared in threat.

Mark jumped from the recliner, chased after Rocky, and grabbed his collar, his other hand on his holster as he called out, "Identify yourself."

"It's me, Jax," he heard from the other side of the metal door as Natalie joined him, standing just behind them.

"*Setz*," he instructed, and Rocky immediately sat, but continued to growl even after Mark said, "Come in."

Jackson cautiously opened the door, peeking in to make sure Rocky was contained before entering. After he confirmed that, he walked in, and Rocky, apparently seeing someone familiar, stopped his rumbling.

"Good morning. You both look like you got some rest," Jackson said, and his keen gaze skipped over them, possibly searching for signs of something else.

"Couch was comfy," Natalie immediately said to dispel where he was going.

"So was the recliner," Mark chimed in, hopefully ending Jackson's worry that anything untoward had happened.

"I've got good news. Ryder was able to rush that DNA test, and we got a hit from CODIS," Jackson said and ambled into the space, a file folder in his hand.

"I'll go make some coffee," Mark said, and was heading to the kitchen when Jackson slapped the file folder against Mark's chest.

"I'll do that. Why don't you and Natalie go over the perp's rap sheet."

Mark grabbed it and walked to the kitchen table, and once she joined him and sat, he did the same and opened the file.

Earl Joinerz. Multiple arrests, some minor. The big one that had landed him in WITSEC was the murder of a DEA agent committed by a motorcycle gang. Joinerz had testified against the leader of the gang in exchange for immunity and witness protection.

Both Rossi and Rogers were involved with Joinerz's security.

"It's good to know what we're up against, but it doesn't help eliminate either Rossi or Rogers as a suspect," Natalie said, which was exactly what he was thinking.

"It doesn't," he said with a frustrated sigh and raked his fingers through his hair.

Jackson ambled over and placed mugs with coffee in front of them.

"Thanks," both Natalie and he said at the same time.

"I agree, although it strikes me that as the junior agent, Rogers might be the one responsible for the everyday things associated with Joinerz's protection," Jackson said and sipped his coffee.

"WHICH MAKES HIM our more likely suspect," Natalie said and wrapped her hands around the warm mug, which helped to chase away the slight nip of morning.

The fire had gone out during the night, and her feet were bare on the natural stone floor. Her makeshift pajamas of a sweatshirt, T-shirt, and sweats did little to keep her comfortable.

But her chill wasn't just about the morning air and stone.

"We need to do something to end this, and I'm all for rolling the dice and reaching out to Rossi," she said despite her worries about the situation.

Jackson narrowed his gaze, scrutinizing her. "By reach out, you mean—"

"Mark and I go see Rossi. We lay our cards on the table and set up a sting to nail Rogers," Natalie said without hesitation, determined to end the risk to her and, more importantly, to Amanda.

A long and possibly stunned silence followed.

She looked up from her mug and the file folder to Jackson, and then to Mark, who was sitting next to her.

"That's a big risk," Jackson said, the features of his handsome face hard, almost like chiseled stone.

"It was a risk to pose as Amanda also, but it's one I'm willing to take," she said, certain of her decision.

"But what if we're not willing to let you do that?" Mark said.

He immediately realized what a mistake that had been when she raised both brows in defiance and in a deadly cold tone said, "You're not the boss of me."

That silence came again, tense. Chillier than the morning air. Solemn, like the quiet of a funeral.

But then Jackson said, "He's not, but for now, I am."

"I was given a job to do, and I need to do it," she argued, wanting to complete the assignment now that she finally remembered what she was supposed to be doing.

"We know that, Natalie. Believe me, we know that," Mark said and laid a hand on her shoulder, offering his support.

"Then you'll help me find a way to end this, before something happens to any of you, Amanda, or me," she pleaded, trying to convince the men that it was time to be on the offensive.

Jackson and Mark shared a long look before Mark said, "The information we have from CPS leans toward Rogers being our prime suspect."

"If we can rely on that—" Natalie began, but Jackson cut her off.

"They've been right before. I trust them without hesitation," he said.

With a dip of her head, she said, "Okay. Let's plan our next steps."

Chapter Twenty-Three

Rossi stared hard at his two marshals, disgusted by their lack of progress.

"Am I to understand that you've checked out every conceivable place that either CPS or Whitaker could have stashed Amanda and come up with nothing?" he said, voice rising in volume as his anger built.

"We identified several shell companies and Williams and I have visited each one, but they were all empty," Rogers said and glanced in his colleague's direction, as if seeking confirmation while also avoiding Rossi's gaze.

Williams nodded and said, "All empty."

"What about any police or Whitaker locations?" Rossi pressed, needing to know they'd exhausted every lead.

"I checked those locations. All empty, but there was evidence that a shooting had taken place at a home not far from the police station. From the information I got from witnesses, it seems like a drive-by," Rogers advised, gaze downcast as he provided his report.

"A drive-by? In a town like Regina?" Rossi said, dissatisfied with his agent's answer.

Rogers finally looked up. "Violence is possible anywhere," Rogers said, his tone defensive, but then he did a slight shrug and added, "I think someone thought they had Alonso there and tried to take her out."

A harsh laugh exploded from him. "You think? That's all your years of training are telling you?"

Embarrassed color flooded the other man's face. "Alonso got cold feet and is long gone," Rogers said, but his tone lacked real conviction.

Rossi nailed the other man with his gaze, scrutinizing him carefully and not liking what he saw.

Besides the bright red across his neck and face, Rogers rocked back and forth on his heels and fidgeted with some change in a pants pocket.

Which reminded him of the BOLO he'd heard over the police scanner that morning.

"Both of you hold out your hands," he said, not wanting to miss anything or give Rogers a clue that he was hesitant about him.

"You think one of us is the person wanted by that BOLO?" Williams challenged, clearly having heard the bulletin as well.

"I think that since Alonso disappeared under your watch, I have to consider every possible angle. Please show me your hands," he said, hating that he had to do it, but the story about Alonso running away wasn't passing muster.

The men did as asked, bringing their hands forward so that he could examine them. He didn't fail to notice that Rogers's hands trembled as he did so, despite there being no sign of any injury.

With a nod, he said, "Good. I'm assuming that BOLO that went out has something to do with Alonso's disappearance. Rogers, check in with any hospital or urgent care center within a thirty-mile radius of Denver. Williams, do the same thing for the Regina area. Report back to me by twelve hundred hours."

"10-4," both men responded briskly and hurried out of the hotel room Rossi was using as base camp during the protection detail.

Not that they'd been all that good at protecting Alonso.

Since he did not doubt that Whitaker had her, he also did not doubt that the drive-by shooting a few blocks away from the stationhouse had been intended to take out Alonso.

Violence of that kind would be extremely rare in a town like Regina. Not that it couldn't happen, but it was truly unlikely.

Which left him with a choice he'd rather not make if Alonso was to testify in two days.

He picked his cell phone up from the bedside table, ready to dial Whitaker, but the police chief was saving him the trouble of making the first move.

"Whitaker," he almost barked in answer.

"Good morning to you, too, Marshal Rossi," Whitaker said, sounding way too chipper, which only ramped up his frustration and anger.

"Cut to the chase, Chief. I've got a lot to do," he said, thinking that besides swinging around the police station to see what was happening, he'd take a trip to the various sites that Williams and Rogers had supposedly checked and get his own read of the situation.

"Well, I hope that I can save you some time," Whitaker said, seemingly unaffected by his sour mood.

"Get to the point," he said from behind gritted teeth, tired of games.

"I need you to come to the police station ASAP. I have some information that might help you find Alonso," he said nonchalantly, as if inviting him to share a coffee and doughnut. Albeit a delicious doughnut.

"Are you going to admit you have her in custody?" he asked.

"I can help you catch the person who took her," the chief said, voice calm and steady.

Way more calm and steady than Rogers had been that morning.

"I'll see you in fifteen," he said and hung up, not wanting

to give Whitaker the satisfaction of knowing he was calling the shots now.

That loss of power grated on him, but not as much as the thought that one of his team was involved in Alonso's disappearance.

Especially since his gut was telling him Rogers might be the one responsible.

He could no longer protect his team member while at the same time understanding why he might have been tempted to either let Alonso run or make sure she didn't testify.

Rogers's daughter's illness had changed his marshal. He'd become careless, likely distracted by all that was going on.

But dirty? Rossi wondered, rushing out of his room to get to the meeting with Whitaker.

As he slipped into his car for the drive, the little voice in his head chastised him.

What would you do for a million dollars? Or to save a child's life?

He couldn't find an answer to that annoying voice.

Instead, he hit the gas and raced to the meeting with Whitaker.

HE LOOKED A lot older than he did in his official photo, as if he carried the weight of the world on his shoulders.

Maybe he did, Natalie thought as she watched Rossi enter the interview room from the observation area.

Whitaker followed him in a second later, and there couldn't have been a greater contrast between the two men, and not just because of age.

There was a slight swagger in Jackson's walk that said he was in control, but surprisingly, his tone was amicable as he laid a coffee and doughnut before the other man.

"It's good to see you, Marshal Rossi," he said as if this was just a friendly visit.

"Let's cut to the chase, Whitaker," Rossi said, but didn't hesitate to reach for the chocolate-glazed doughnut.

"Let's," Jackson replied and looked directly at the two-way mirror.

A gentle touch came on her shoulder as Mark squeezed it reassuringly.

"Are you ready?" he asked softly.

Am I? she wondered and looked over her shoulder at him. "Ready as I'll ever be."

He trailed his hand down to hers and twined his fingers with hers. "Let's go, then."

With a nod, she walked out of the observation room, hand in hand with Mark.

They paused at the interview room door and knocked.

At Jackson's "Come in," they dropped their hands, and Mark slipped in front of her.

"Just in case," he said, still worried that Rossi might be the one who wanted Amanda gone.

She didn't think that and yet still worried that Mark was putting himself in danger for her sake.

But she didn't dwell on that fear as he pushed into the room.

She followed barely a breath later and closed the door.

Rossi paused with the doughnut halfway to his mouth.

His eyes widened the barest bit before he finally took a bite, chewed slowly, and swallowed before he said, "Well, well. Why am I not surprised?"

Before any of them could say a word, Rossi pushed on. "I could have both you and your sergeant arrested. Obstruction. Interfering with a federal agent—"

"Only then you would have to admit that you lost control of your team. That one of them went rogue. You prepared to do that and risk everything you've worked for?" Mark immediately countered.

A bark of a laugh escaped Rossi. "Everything I worked for?" he said and nailed Natalie with a hard-eyed glance.

"You had a big deposit into one of your accounts recently. Any explanation?" Natalie said.

"I see you did your homework. My wife's mother lived to the ripe old age of one hundred and three and passed a few months ago. The money was a settlement from her estate," he said, and before she could say anything else, he added, "You can check it out with my attorney if you like. We're lucky to have that after what you did. There isn't much left of what I worked for thanks to your fraud."

"But despite that, you were willing to protect me?" Natalie said, scrutinizing the man to see if they could trust him.

He lifted his broad shoulders in a careless shrug. "Not much left but honor. Duty. Things you wouldn't know a thing about," he said, and looked over at Jackson. "Could we move this along? I need to get Alonso back into custody."

"It's not that simple, Marshal Rossi," Natalie said, and at Jackson's nod, she continued.

"I'm not Amanda Alonso. I'm her twin sister, Natalie. I'm a Denver homicide detective."

Surprise and doubt registered on Rossi's bulldog features. He squinted as he examined her and shook his head.

Glaring at Jackson and Mark, he said, "Is this some kind of sick joke? Are you all in cahoots to get her money?"

Mark rushed to the table and slammed his hands on his desktop. "Do you think we don't have the same honor and duty that you do? If you do, you are sadly mistaken."

"And you'd be ignoring what you know in your gut, namely that someone on your team is responsible for Amanda's disappearance," Jackson said, all friendliness gone from his voice.

"You can confirm what I'm telling you with Maya Freeman and Walter Allen. I think you know who they are," Natalie said, cold dripping from her voice with the marshal's accusations at the men who had saved her life.

All color fled Rossi's face, and his hand trembled as he reached for his coffee. "I know who they are," he said, his defeat obvious.

To Jackson's credit, he addressed the older man respectfully and with real sympathy as he said, "We're not your enemies, Jack. We want to help you catch whoever did this. We want to work with you, not against you."

"You could have done that from the start," Rossi immediately shot back, but it lacked much bite.

MARK FELT FOR the other man. He truly did. He couldn't imagine how he'd feel if he thought someone on their squad had betrayed them.

He sat down kitty-corner to the man and said, "We think we know who's gone rogue. But I think you know as well."

Rossi dropped his head, almost in denial, but then a single word escaped him. "Rogers."

Mark nodded. "Yes, Rogers. We don't have much to arrest him yet, but it's a start. Together we can connect the dots."

The older man nodded and, in a tired voice, said, "Both Williams and Rogers were assigned to check out possible locations where Alonso might be."

"We had breaches at three locations," Natalie said, and provided him the information, inviting him to add what he knew.

"Rogers was the agent responsible for checking those locations," Rossi admitted weakly and then sipped his coffee.

"Thank you for that information," Mark said and laid a hand on the other man's shoulder, offering him support. As Jackson passed over a file folder, Mark opened it, removed Earl Joinerz's rap sheet, and placed it in front of the older man.

"Does he look familiar?" he asked.

"You know that he does. Rogers and I were responsible for

arranging his protection, maybe four or five years ago," Rossi said and pushed the papers back in Mark's direction.

"Williams had nothing to do with Joinerz?" he pressed, just to make sure they weren't letting tunnel vision possibly focus on the wrong person.

Rossi shook his head. "None. Williams only came onto my team about a year ago."

"Based on this, as well as Rogers's family issues, would you say we're right that he's our main suspect?" Natalie said, tone sympathetic, and her gaze almost pleading with the marshal.

Rossi took a deep breath that expanded his broad chest, held it inordinately long, and then slowly released it past gritted teeth. "I don't want to believe it, but… I've been worried about Rogers for months. Ever since they diagnosed his daughter with that cancer, he's been distracted. Who wouldn't be? I tried to cover for him as best as I could."

"You wouldn't be human if you didn't feel for him," Natalie said and reached out to grasp the man's hand as it rested by the file folder.

Rossi slipped his hand from beneath hers, clearly uncomfortable with her commiseration. With his other hand, he rubbed his chin, deep in thought.

The man remained silent for long minutes, but then Mark pushed on.

"We all feel for him, but as much as we might not like it, we have a job to do. We need to eliminate the threat to Amanda and find out who's behind it."

"How do you propose we do that?" Rossi asked.

Chapter Twenty-Four

"I'm going to become bait," Natalie said without hesitation.

Rossi immediately shouted out, "No way. You may not be Amanda, but I'm not going to let you risk your life."

"It's the only way Amanda can testify," Natalie urged.

"That's only two days away," Rossi began, and Natalie quickly shut him down.

"More reason to act now."

Rossi shook his head and rubbed his chin again, but with a tired sigh, he finally acquiesced. "What do you want to do?"

"We need to draw Rogers out, and the only way to do that is for him to try and take Natalie again," Mark said and did a quick peek in her direction. "I'm not a fan of that either, but we'll take every possible precaution to avoid anyone getting hurt."

"Even Rogers?" Rossi asked and lifted his salt-and-pepper brows in question.

"We don't want anyone hurt, and that includes Rogers," Mark said.

"How do we do that? If he's desperate, and we have to assume he is because of his daughter's illness, he's bound to use force since the clock is ticking," Rossi said, worry apparent in the set of his features and the slight upward toss of his hands, as if in surrender.

Natalie nodded and said, "You're right. That's why we'll all be wearing body armor—"

"Which won't stop a bullet to that pretty head," Rossi said and tapped a spot dead center of his forehead.

His words made her blood run cold, even though it was something they'd all considered the night before as they'd made some preliminary plans. But as a cop, she faced that kind of risk daily.

"It's part of the job," she said with a shrug.

Rossi narrowed his gaze and stared at her hard. "Have you ever seen someone die, Detective? Watched the life fade from their eyes?"

"Marshal Rossi—" she interjected, but he didn't stop.

"Did you ever pull the trigger? Killed someone?" he said.

"ENOUGH!" MARK BARKED OUT. "That's not going to help."

"Maybe not, but I want to make sure we all keep that in mind while we finalize this plan," the marshal said and peered at everyone at the table.

"We'll keep that in mind," Jackson said, then stood and walked over to one side of the room and a whiteboard where they'd laid out the preliminary details of the plan developed the night before with the assistance of Crooked Pass Security.

He flipped the whiteboard around so that Rossi could see it and motioned for Mark to continue.

Mark appreciated the confidence that his friend and boss had shown in him during the case. He walked over to the board and said, "CPS will assist us whenever we put this plan into action. They'll also run our final plan through their predictive program to identify any weaknesses so we can address them."

"You think some fancy AI program will know more than experienced cops?" Rossi challenged.

"We think that we'll use all resources available to keep everyone safe," Mark said, and before Rossi could challenge anything else, he ran down the preliminary plan.

Rossi pulled out a pen and portfolio and scratched out notes as Mark detailed how Natalie would exit the station, exposing herself to an attack.

"What about Joinerz?" Rossi pressed and dropped his pen onto the pad of paper.

"Joinerz was injured in the last attack. Both arms. A dog bite on one. Natalie likely broke bones in the other arm. Program says he's likely out of commission, which means we're only dealing with Rogers," Mark advised.

Rossi tipped his head from side to side. "Unless Rogers brought in another felon to assist."

"That's a possibility, but with so little time left, what are the odds he can bring in someone else? Not to mention he's got to pay them, and that's fewer dollars for his daughter's treatments," Natalie pointed out.

"And the predictive program confirms the probability is low based on all the variables," Jackson advised.

Rossi huffed out a dismissive breath. "What else does the program say?"

"The program says it's low probability that Rogers will try to take Natalie out on the steps of the police station, but if he did decide to do that..." Mark began and laid out the scenario worked on with CPS, namely, the attack with a single shooter moving down Main Street.

"Rogers would be driving and shooting. High risk for everyone involved," Mark said, and with a big red whiteboard marker, he put an X through that portion of the board.

"Let's say you and the program are right. What's the next thing you have up there?" Rossi said and gestured to the board.

"We get Natalie in a car headed to a safe house in Denver. That's an hour drive, mostly along major roadways, except for two areas," Mark said, and gestured to the map. "First spot is here in Regina and the short distance along this minor county road. Second is once we get off in this Denver suburb."

"We're leaning toward the attack taking place here, in Regina," Natalie said and joined Mark at the whiteboard. Circling a position with a finger, she said, "There are way too many cops we can call for backup in Denver. Not as many here, which means—"

"Either Joinerz or Rogers is going to create some kind of distraction to pull our cops away," Jackson said and sighed. "It won't take much. A fight at the supermarket. Car crash on Main Street. We're not a big department."

"That's why CPS is going to lend us one of their agents with a trained K-9 in case a foot pursuit is necessary," Mark added.

Rossi laid a hand on his mouth and rubbed his upper lip with his index finger, considering the analysis carefully. "Let's assume you're right. There's a weakness for how long along the route?"

"Let's display it on the monitor," Mark said and moved the whiteboard out of the way to reveal a large monitor on the wall. He grabbed a remote that had been sitting on the marker storage bar of the whiteboard and turned it on.

Jackson opened his laptop, and with a few keystrokes, he displayed a detailed map where several possible routes out of Regina had been identified.

ROSSI PEERED AT the map, not as familiar with the area as Mark and Jackson. Waving an index finger around, he said, "I assume those numbers in red aren't route numbers."

"No, they're not. They're probabilities—"

"Where he'll attack?" he asked despite his reticence to rely on any kind of fancy program to do police work.

"How we can make it cleanly to the main highway. Very low probability he'll attack there. Too many people and too hard to isolate us in the traffic," Mark said, and gestured to one route.

"This is our best chance to get to the highway, but if the idea is to draw in Rogers..." Natalie stopped, voice trailing off.

Rossi pointed to one route. "You take the route where it's easiest for him to attack and neutralize him."

Mark gestured to several areas along the streets. "Natalie and I would be in one car. Jackson following in another. Plus, one CPS agent and one Regina squad car."

"That's it?" Rossi said incredulously.

"You can bring up the rear or ask Williams to join us, if you want. That's two more bodies. But honestly, having too many vehicles involved might scare off Rogers," Natalie said.

The detective wasn't wrong. Even though Rogers had been distracted lately, he would likely pick up on multiple tails.

"You're right. Too many cooks. I'll hang back once you leave and see if I spot Rogers," he said and waved for them to continue.

With a nod, the young cop laid out the route, the possible ways Rogers might come at them, as well as their response. He hated to admit it, but it all made sense, and he was impressed with what a supposedly small-town police department had managed to put together.

But then again, they had the assistance of Crooked Pass Security, and they were well-connected and highly accomplished.

As Dillon finished the rundown, Rossi said, "Okay. When do we lure Rogers into this trap?"

Dillon peered at Natalie and then at Jackson. When the police chief nodded, Mark said, "If Amanda is supposed to testify in two days, we have to do it this afternoon."

NATALIE PULLED THE Velcro fasteners tight on the ballistic body armor. It would protect her against any bullets hitting her torso, but not a head shot, as Rossi had warned that morning.

But it was a risk she had to take. It wouldn't be the first time nor her last.

When she finished, she swiveled to look at Mark, who was

likewise dressing in the protective garment. With a final zip as he reset the fasteners, he was done and met her gaze.

"Ready?" he asked.

She sucked in a steadying breath and laid a hand on her stomach to quell the nervous flutters there. "Ready."

Mark nodded. "Okay. Let's check in with Rossi and Jackson. See if they've triangulated where Rogers is and if we're a go."

Natalie glanced at her watch. "It's been at least an hour since Rossi called him to say that I was being brought in. Should be time enough for Rogers to be back from Denver."

"Should be, and if he's here, he's ignoring Rossi's instructions to check the hospitals," Mark said.

As she walked past him to the door, he took hold of her hand to draw her close. She leaned against him, burying her head against his chest, and he slipped an arm around her waist.

"We're going to be okay," she said, trying to allay his fears as well as her own.

"We are. And after..." he said, asking the question they hadn't voiced but knew they would have to address.

Offering him a sad smile, she said, "We'll deal with the after after."

A half smile with one of those engaging dimples drifted across his lips. "Okay, we'll deal with the after after."

With a final hug, they hurried from the police station's armory to the interview area that had become their war room with the arrival of Diego Rodriguez, the CPS K-9 agent.

Diego was a familiar face in Regina since he'd been an officer on the force over a year earlier and was helping them train and develop Regina PD's K-9 Division.

Jackson was in the room with Rossi, Diego, and Millie Alvarez, a recently promoted detective and one of their sharpest. He was assigning them positions along the route they planned to take.

After he finished identifying the spots, Jackson motioned

to her and said, "This is Amanda Alonso, our chief witness in the fraud case against David Peterson. Our goal is to move her safely to Denver, where she is set to testify tomorrow."

As he spoke, Diego raised a brow, clearly aware of her real identity, unlike Millie. But he said nothing, aware of the need to keep the ruse going as long as possible.

"We've confirmed that Rogers is in the area contrary to the instructions he was given by Marshal Rossi," Jackson said and motioned to Rossi to continue the briefing.

"Unfortunately, based on all available evidence, Rogers is our prime suspect in the recent attacks, along with Earl Joinerz, a convicted felon in our WITSEC program," Rossi said and handed Diego and Alvarez photos of the two men.

"We believe Joinerz may create some kind of disturbance to draw members of the Regina Police Department away from the station and the vehicle with Alonso. You do not move from your locations unless instructed by either me or Chief Whitaker," Rossi said and turned the briefing back to Jackson.

"We want you to take your positions ASAP. Once you're in place, use the comms devices you've been provided to keep us advised. Rogers is likely listening in to the police scanner, so do not use your police radios for communications."

"10-4," both officers said, and at Jackson's nod, they hurried off to reach their assigned locations.

After they were gone, Jackson handed Mark and her communications devices. He also handed her a holster with a police-issued Glock. "I assume you know how to use that."

She made sure the safety was on, efficiently ejected the magazine, and also checked that there wasn't already a bullet in the chamber. Satisfied, she put the clip back in and holstered the weapon.

"I guess that's a 'yes,'" Jackson said with a laugh.

"Thanks for this, although I hope not to use it," Natalie said and clipped the holster to the waistband of her jeans.

"We all hope the same thing," Mark said, and likewise checked his weapon.

"As soon as Diego and Millie are in position, we'll move," Jackson said, his face a mask of stone.

"10-4," both Mark and she said, and the nervous flutters in her stomach intensified to the point that she almost vomited. She swallowed back the bile and started to pace, burning away the nervous energy making her physically ill.

Chapter Twenty-Five

Mark wanted to offer comfort as she strode back and forth across the width of the room, but held back.

She needed to prepare for the assignment in the ways she knew best.

So did he.

He hurried to the monitor displaying the map with the route they'd decided on to trap Rogers, wanting to memorize every aspect of it so he would be prepared for any attack.

Jackson joined him a second later, arms across his chest as he stood next to Mark.

"You ready?" he asked, but didn't look his way, his focus on the map.

Mark nodded and said, "I am."

Jackson's head swiveled to track Natalie's nervous movements in the room.

Mark didn't wait for his boss and friend to ask the obvious. "She's ready, too," he said, certain that Natalie could handle whatever would come their way.

The chirp of Jackson's phone kept him from pushing.

"Whitaker," his boss answered and listened. With a dip of his head, he said, "Let me put you on speaker."

When he did so, they all gathered around and Jackson said, "Can you repeat that, Officer Adams?"

"I've got eyes on Joinerz. He's got an air cast on one arm

and what looks like a bandage on the other. He's at Luna Marketplace," Adams reported.

"Good. Keep him in your sights. He's probably going to create some kind of disturbance. When he does, call it in on the radio like you normally would. Ask for backup. Officer Parker will assist in getting Joinerz in custody. Got that?"

"10-4, Chief," Adams said and ended the call.

"The pieces are falling into place," Mark said, pleased that their plan seemed to be coming together.

Rossi wasn't as enthusiastic. "Still a lot of pieces that could go missing."

Mark ignored the older man whose pessimistic expression reminded him of a bulldog a friend had once had. Nothing they ever did could make that dog look happy.

He suspected that Rossi was much the same, but then again, Rossi had a lot to be unhappy about.

A retirement fund almost emptied, and a rogue agent on his detail.

But Mark wasn't going to dwell on possible failures. He was going to visualize getting Rogers, peacefully, and ending the threat to Amanda.

And after that? the little voice in his head asked.

He met Natalie's gaze. *The after after.* He was eager to explore what would happen between them when the threat had been eliminated.

THE MOMENT WAS BUILDING, Natalie thought, and slipped her hand into Mark's.

"It'll be time soon," she said and offered a gentle squeeze.

"It is time," Jackson said, and Rossi echoed his agreement.

"Rogers has been in the area for some time. He's probably got eyes on the station by now."

"Let's confirm Diego and Millie are in position," Jackson said and texted both officers.

As a series of chirps followed, Jackson nodded and said, "They're ready."

With a look in her direction, he said, "I'll go first and make sure it's clear. We have a cruiser located directly in front of the station. Mark will load you into the back, but first…"

He grabbed handcuffs from his utility belt and held them up. "Let's make this look real. They'll be loose enough for you to slip off."

Natalie held out her hands, and he cuffed her. The metal was cold against her wrists and heavy, but Jackson did as promised, and didn't tighten them. Still, from a distance, they would be convincing enough to anyone watching.

Her hair was up in a topknot, and as he'd done numerous times, Mark slipped on a ball cap to offer some disguise.

She murmured her thanks, and with Jackson leading the way, Mark took her arm for the perp walk through the station and down the stairs. Rocky was at his side while Rossi brought up the rear, so close she imagined she could feel his breath stir the fine hairs at the nape of her neck.

A couple of officers were in the bullpen to handle calls, and their heads swiveled as they walked through.

At the front door, Jackson paused and gestured for them to step away out of possible gunfire reach.

She held her breath as he exited, aware of the risk. Hating it since Jackson had a wife and baby waiting for him.

"All clear," he said and hurried to get into the lead cruiser for their trip, not that they expected to make it out of Regina without incident if their analysis and the program were accurate.

Mark clicked his tongue and sent Rocky on ahead a second before they rushed down the steps.

Her gaze darted all around, taking in the scene. Looking for any signs of Rogers or anything else that might be suspicious.

Nada, she thought as Mark quickly commanded Rocky into the back, and he urged her in.

The door closed with a resounding thud, and Mark rushed around to the driver's side.

"We slipped the Glock beneath the passenger seat," he said as he snapped on his lights and pulled out, following Jackson's cruiser down Main Street and leaving Rossi on the front side-walk, staring after them.

She turned as they got a block away and watched as he slipped into his sedate black sedan to bring up the rear.

Satisfied they were clear, she slipped off the cuffs, bent, and recovered the Glock.

MARK CAUGHT HER motion in the rearview mirror.

She was armed and ready, and so was he as he kept his head on a swivel, alert for anything that seemed out of the ordinary.

Ahead of him, Jackson detoured from what would normally be the quickest route, namely straight down Main Street, to a county road by the lake that eventually connected to the high-way to Denver.

They'd eliminated that route for fear of collateral damage to pedestrians and residents if Rogers intercepted them anywhere along Main Street.

Instead, Jackson immediately turned off onto a residential side street that fed into a road past mostly light industrial build-ings on one side and a stream that fed the lake on the other.

The probabilities said Rogers wouldn't risk an attack on the residential street, but once they were on the other road…

Jackson paused before the turn, waiting for a truck to pass and a break in traffic large enough so that Mark could follow. Maybe Rossi as well, Mark thought as his black sedan appeared in the rearview mirror.

Diego and Millie were positioned along that road at key spots, ready to hem Rogers in if he attacked.

No, not *if*, Mark told himself. *When*.

"You okay back there?" he said as he started the turn and glimpsed Natalie in the side-view mirror.

"Rocky and I are both good," she said and rubbed the dog's head.

He normally would have harnessed his partner, but he wanted him free in case of an attack or pursuit.

"We're in the danger zone now," he said, since there were several side streets that fed along this road, giving Rogers ample opportunities to take action.

They had barely gone a few blocks when a flash of light and the sound of a racing action warned that trouble had arrived.

ROSSI SHOUTED OUT a curse as a pickup truck barreled out of a nearby parking lot and into the side of the cruiser with Mark and Natalie.

Metal crunched and glass flew into the air as the pickup pushed the cruiser across the opposite lane of traffic and onto the short embankment along the stream.

The cruiser tipped precariously onto its side and then, with a final push, slid sideways into the water.

JACKSON JERKED TO a stop and was about to reverse to prevent Rogers from escaping, but suddenly his radio started squawking that a fight had broken out at the Luna Marketplace between Joinerz and two store clerks.

"We're at Tenth and County Road 231. Move in, Diego and Millie. Adams and Parker, get Joinerz in custody," he said into the radio, trusting his team to handle the situation as he jumped from his cruiser.

He drew his weapon and raced toward where the pickup sat at an odd angle on the road.

As he approached, the driver's-side door flew open, and a bloodied Rogers stumbled from the pickup, gun drawn.

"Drop it," Jackson called out just as Rossi came at Rogers from the opposite side, weapon drawn.

"Don't do it, Mike. Think of Julie and Sandy. You don't want them to remember you for this," Rossi said, trying to appeal to the man.

Rogers paused, weapon still held high, and said, "You don't understand, Jack. I need the money Peterson promised me. I have to finish this job."

Jackson worried that he already had done just that, since the cruiser with Mark, Natalie, and Rocky was sitting in several feet of water, with no signs of any activity.

He had a choice to make at that moment.

Help his friends trapped in the partially submerged car or continue to hold Rogers at bay.

As he met Rossi's gaze from across the distance separating them, he knew there was only one thing he could do.

For a second, everything had gone black.

But then ice-cold water woke him and he knew he had to act.

He was sideways, totally underwater. He fumbled with the release as he fought for a breath, but inhaled water instead.

Pounding came against the metal barrier with the back seat.

"Mark. Get out, Mark," Natalie shouted, and it came as if from far away.

He turned his head, searching for the surface of the water, but couldn't see it.

He didn't have much time left as the cold of the water filled him, and circles danced in his gaze.

His fingers grew heavy, leaden as he tried to push the seat belt release.

Such a simple thing, and it's going to kill me.

Natalie had been stunned, tossed across the back seat and into Rocky as the pickup had T-boned them onto the soft slope near the stream.

The tipping of the car onto its side had seemed to happen in slow motion, and she'd grabbed hold of Rocky to try to protect the dog as they'd tumbled into the cold waters of the stream.

The rear driver's-side door was pinned shut. Her back door had taken most of the damage and wouldn't open, but luckily, the window had shattered.

She kicked away the last bits of glass and helped Rocky up into the opening.

The dog immediately hopped out, and she followed, boosting herself through the window to find Jackson there.

"Mark's trapped in his seat," she said, and Jackson went into action, but the wreck had damaged the front passenger door as well.

A quick look toward the road revealed that Rossi and Rogers were standing there, weapons pointed at each other in an impasse.

"Help Rossi. I'll get Mark out," she said, and didn't hesitate to slip in through the broken window to reach Mark.

The water was ice cold, and Mark was no longer moving.

She reached down, located the seat belt release, and pushed hard, the button slippery from the water. The cold of the water numbed her fingers. With a second hard push, it opened.

The seat belt floated away, and Mark's body bobbed lifelessly in the water.

She pulled his head above water. His face was pale. Too pale, she thought as she struggled to get him to the window.

She managed to get one leg against the column of the steering wheel and push them upward.

But as strong and determined as she was, Mark was dead weight, making it impossible to get him through the opening.

Please, please, please, Lord, she pleaded as she held him close and rubbed her hands across his back, hoping it would rouse him.

The Lord answered her prayers, as a heartbeat later, she heard, "Let me get him, Natalie."

Diego was instantly at the window, grabbing hold of Mark's shirt and hauling him halfway out. With her pushing from beneath and one final jerk, Mark slid out the window, and Diego gently lowered him to the ground.

She was shaking from the cold of the water and adrenaline as she stood there, taking in everything around her.

Rogers was on his knees, hands on his head, surrounded by Jackson, Rossi, and Sergeant Alvarez.

Diego was performing CPR on Mark.

She dropped to her knees opposite him and said, "What can I do?"

"I gave him the rescue breaths. Now thirty compressions and then I need you to do two more breaths," he said, while he pumped Mark's chest deeply.

Mark's head had flopped to the side, and she gently tilted it back, ready to act, but he suddenly spat out mouthfuls of water. A few coughs, and he was breathing on his own and opening his eyes.

"Did we get him?" he asked, voice hoarse.

"We did," she said, then bent and kissed him as the sound of an ambulance siren filled the air.

Chapter Twenty-Six

Rossi and Jackson had taken Rogers and Joinerz into custody and alerted the relevant authorities that Amanda was now safe to testify.

Rossi had convinced Rogers to turn against Peterson in exchange for his putting in a good word to get Rogers a lesser sentence. It had helped that Sophie and Robbie Whitaker had offered to assist with the money that Rogers needed for his daughter's treatment.

Natalie and Mark had gone to the hospital to be checked out. Despite the powerful collision, they'd suffered only a few bruises here and there. Even luckier, Mark seemed to have no lingering effects from his near drowning and had refused an overnight stay in the hospital as a precaution.

Plus, they both had recognized that it was time for the after after.

She had driven them back to Jackson's parents' lakeside cabin since that was the only home she had until her return to Denver once Amanda testified. For the moment, as far as the world knew, she was still Amanda and in a Regina safe house.

But as they walked in hand in hand and closed the door, they knew it was finally time to explore the attraction that had been simmering between them for days, and luckily, Diego had offered to watch Rocky for the night so they could be alone.

Mark led her to the fireplace and quickly got a fire going. "I still feel the cold of that water," he said as he rose and slipped his arms around her.

"I think I know just what to do to make you forget that," she said, and her fingers flew across the buttons of his uniform shirt, quickly baring him to her gaze.

There were an assortment of bruises where the seat belt had dug into him, and she skimmed her hands across them lightly, conscious of how close she'd come to losing him.

He cupped her chin with his thumb and forefinger and applied gentle pressure to tilt her gaze to his. "Don't think about that."

"I can't help it. We should have listened to the program warning about that stream," she said, then traced the lean muscles of his midsection and reached down to his belt buckle. It jangled as she undid it and let it drop loose before she stroked her hand down his hard length.

"Maybe, but I know one thing that program can't do," he said, and nibbled his way along her jaw to a sensitive spot just behind her ear.

"What's that?" she asked breathlessly, already anticipating where this was leading.

"This," he said as he gently lowered her to the soft rug in front of the fireplace and covered her with his muscled body.

The fire had caught quickly, radiating warmth across them as they quickly undressed. But it was nothing like the heat of their bodies as gentle touches soon became urgent, needing more. Needing to be joined as passion burned brighter than the flames licking at the wood in the fireplace.

She had been straddling him, riding along his length as he kissed and caressed her breasts, but suddenly he rolled, trapping her beneath him.

"Are you sure?" he asked, ever the gentleman, asking her permission.

"I've never been more sure."

He took only a moment to slip on protection, and then he was poised at her center again.

She welcomed him in, joining with him. Moving against him as they rose ever higher, kissing and caressing each other until, with one final thrust, he took them over.

After, they lay together in front of the fire, savoring their hard-earned peace until Mark leaned on an elbow and peered at her, the green of his eyes as dark as a forest at night. His smiling lips with that engaging dimple tempting her.

"I know this assignment will be done soon, but I was hoping you might stay in Regina a little longer," he said and skimmed a lock of hair away from her face.

"I have some vacation time coming," she said with a grin as she cupped the back of his head and urged him down for a kiss.

"What happens after that?" he asked as he answered her kiss, and she rolled him onto his back.

"After that? I hear Regina is still hiring," she said and lay across his body, her head pillowed on his chest.

"Do you think a big-city detective like you could be happy in a small town like Regina?" he asked.

She raised her head and skimmed her gaze across his features, golden from the firelight. "I don't know. Think you can convince me to stay?" she teased.

He rolled, trapping her beneath him. Bending his head, he kissed that spot behind her ear again and whispered, "How about I show you just how convincing I can be?"

She laughed and kissed the side of his face. "I think I'd like that."

* * * * *